When
THE **Whistle**
Blows

By

SCOTT STAERKEL

ISBN: 1-4033-3915-5 (e-book)
ISBN: 1-4033-3916-3 (Paperback)
ISBN: 1-4033-3917-1 (Dustjacket)

This book is printed on acid free paper.

1stBooks - rev. 09/13/02

Acknowledgements

For those who have toiled and suffered under its unbearable weight—this arrow is aimed at the heart filled with hate. As for me, my quiver is full.

I would like to personally thank all those who have recognized and supported me in this work. To my professors who encouraged me; to an agent who recognized its value, to two producers who validated me as a *writer* at a time when I had little self-worth. And not to forget the 5 J's who sometimes had to put up with a tired and cranky dad.

I remember a time when my soul was at rest, when you were beside me, life was so blessed. Then came the storm, and I mourned your last breath. Now I am here, alone with my grief. My dreams lay shattered beneath your feet. Oh how my heart longs to once more hear your voice. But I can't—so I write—to ease my pain—and yours. It is my only choice. Someday I hope to see what you saw and rejoice.

To Jody, John + Family

The Dream is alive and well.

Scott Stanhel

12-16-02

Dedication

This one is for Albert, Cindy, Frances, Orrel, and T.

CONTENTS

CHAPTER ONE

It was mid- August 1964. The dog days of summer had arrived, and with them the sound of cicadas. They were everywhere it seemed. Their chants charged the air. The heat brought them out, and the hotter it got, the louder they seemed to voice their displeasure.

Today, it sure was hot. So it seemed to one lanky brown-haired, blue-eyed 11-year-old boy by the name of Kevin Campbell.

The thermometer on the side of Kevin's house said 106. Kevin swore it was hotter. And as he made his way toward Market Street in search of empty bottles—the droning sound of the cicadas lamenting the stifling heat reminded him of the situation he was now in.

This wasn't exactly how he had planned on spending his Friday afternoon. But with the prospects of no allowance for at least the next four weeks, Kevin thought it seemed to be a reasonable solution to his current dilemma. Namely, he was out of money, it was hot, and he was thirsty.

Kevin tilted his head and wiped the dripping sweat from the side of his widened brow. As he did, his father's stinging upbraiding lingered in his thoughts like the sounds of the cicadas hanging above him in the trees.

"No allowance for a month," his father had sternly told him, "I work too hard for my money to be buying new bedroom windows."

These were hard words for Kevin to swallow. Mainly, because they were true. His dad did work hard for his money, and that fact was beyond dispute.

Nonetheless, as Kevin had reasoned to his father, the broken window wasn't entirely his fault. He wouldn't have hit it, if *it* hadn't moved. But the *bird* had moved, and the window had broken, another fact beyond dispute.

Kevin never thought an errant BB could get him into so much trouble. But it did, and he was—and so for the time being—as his father had told him, "Your allowance will be put to better use!"

The going rate for empty soda pop bottles was two cents. And the heavily- trafficked road beside which Kevin now walked was a perfect place to find them. With his arms nearly full; Kevin scanned the withering grass beside the busy road— hoping to find one more. Up ahead, about a block away he could see Stone's Grocery. It was a small corner store. He could redeem the bottles there.

Famous for its speckled gumballs redeemable for a dime—that is if you were ever lucky enough to get one out of the machine—Stone's grocery was a favorite hangout for the neighborhood kids.

Situated on the corner of 30th and Chestnut Streets, on the edge of the east side of town, Stone's Grocery was a family-owned store. And like so many other places in this small, Mid-western town, Kevin visited it often. So, with five soda pop bottles already collected, and one more in sight, Kevin decided to end his search, and turn them in.

About a mile from where Kevin was paying his penance for the broken window, a small group of neighborhood boys were beginning to gather on a local playground. It was another place familiar to Kevin.

Located in the heart of a lower- middle- class neighborhood—the playground sat next to a red- bricked school named Adam's Elementary. It was complete with swings, slide, and jungle gym.

Sitting next to the playground was a baseball diamond, neatly kept. The diamond opened up to a large and wide grassy field. It was a perfect place to play football. Green leafy towering trees surrounded the field. They were mainly oak and elm.

On this field, a generation of kids had come to play. Many a fierce battle had taken place here. More than a few local legends had been made here.

And not far from that grassy field, about a mile or two to the northeast, was the Champlin refinery. It was a sprawling 640-

3

acre complex jammed- packed with state- of- the- art oil refining equipment. The plant was surrounded by nearly three dozen large, cylindrical oil storage tanks. Each tank was painted white and numbered.

The refinery complex was heavily guarded. It was a 24-hour- a- day secure facility, and the day shift was nearly finished. Judging by the looks on the faces of its workers, the many men were glad it was over. They looked hot and tired as they filed out.

But for one local oil refinery worker by the name of Bill Campbell—one could tell that it was more than just the end of another long hard day's work. It was also the beginning of something new—you could tell by the extra pep in his step as he gathered up his belongings.

He was an athletic man, about 35, and stood about 5 foot 10 inches tall. As he took off his shiny steel hat and wiped the sweat from his tan furrowed brow, his short brown hair glistened in the sun. His eyes were steely blue. His tanned face seemed to highlight them.

Overhead, a high- pitched steam whistle blew out over the refinery. Bill looked up and followed its hollow sound. The echo seemed to last forever as it faded out. And Bill was not alone— the other men working the day shift—wearing their silver steel hats and carrying their black tin lunch pails—looked up too. They also savored its sound.

It was quitting time.

But Bill Campbell and his co-workers weren't the only ones who noticed the sound of the whistle, and its fading echo. It had gotten other people's attention too. For every day, at the same time, for the past 30 years, the tranquil silence of this small town had been broken by the shrill of that whistle.

In fact, every day, whenever that whistle blew—all over town—people would stop and turn their heads. Some would check their watches; others would crane their necks. It was three o'clock; you could almost set your watch by it.

And so, as Bill and the other workers lined up against a tall thin corrugated tin wall, Bill was fifth in line. He wasted little time as he grabbed his time card from the rack, and quickly punched the clock. Behind him, a seemingly endless line of men prepared to do the same.

Firmly clutching the handle of his lunch pail in his right hand, Bill walked down the long narrow pathway leading out of the refinery. And for the moment, only one thought now occupied his mind—*football*—and the start of a new season. He had waited for this day for many months, and now it was here.

Up ahead, Bill could see gate number five and his point of exit. He was only a few minutes from home. And to his right, high above him, as he walked along the black top, he could also see Old Faithful—the seemingly eternal yellow flame burning brightly above the refinery.

He could also see the next shift already hard at work, proving what he often said, "The refinery never sleeps, and its workers seldom rest."

And so it was today, as Bill exited gate number five and walked to his gray 1960 Ford truck. Wearing his hard-hat;

carrying his lunchpail, he almost looked like an astronaut as he emerged through the shimmering heat.

Back at Stone's Grocery, Kevin placed the empty soda pop bottles he had collected onto the counter top, and redeemed them for an ice-cold bottle of Grape Nehi soda and a handful of penny candy.

The woman behind the cash register was always warm and friendly. Kevin liked her a lot. Wearing her traditional horn-rimmed glasses; she smiled at him as she pushed a lone penny back across the formica top.

She watched as Kevin retrieved it and tried his luck at the speckled gumball machine. With a twist of the handle, the gumball fell into the trough. Slowly raising the lid, Kevin bent over, and with one eye closed, peered inside at the contents. The gumball was blue. Kevin sighed a little.

"Better luck next time," the lady said.

Kevin smiled at her and placed the gumball in his mouth.

"Yeah, next time," he said.

As Kevin exited Stone's that hot summer day, and the bell above the door jingled over his head, his thoughts turned elsewhere. Like his father, he too now had but one thing on his mind—*football*. And he wasted little time as he quickly made his way to the playground and joined his friends on the grassy field. When he arrived, the game was already in progress.

Like everyone else on the field that afternoon, the familiar sound of the steam whistle had gotten Kevin's attention too. He too had heard it. Like the rest of the boys, when it had sounded, he had momentarily stopped what he was doing and stretched his neck to the sky. He also knew what time it was.

But at *that* moment, *at that very moment*, a more pressing concern was facing Kevin Campbell. Standing in front of him— on the other side of the ball was Randy Milligan, a rather chubby boy, about five foot two. And the pressure was on—it was fourth down.

And thus, the blue- eyed wonder of Adams Elementary, looked to his left, and then to his right. And with the not too distant memory of the sound of the whistle fading off in his mind, he bent under his center, and barked out his signals.

"Two forty two, Red eleven. Blue twenty-four!"

His boyish voice echoed in the air. Across from Kevin, a small piece of saliva wetted the corner of Randy's mouth. *He almost looked rabid*, Kevin thought.

It was not a pretty sight.

"I'm about to smash your butt," Randy told him with labored breath. Kevin looked his foe in the eye. Somehow he believed him.

Kevin's eyes widened as he bellowed out the remaining count, "Settt, hut, hut!"

As the center snapped the ball, it became readily obvious no one would be a match for Randy Milligan. He easily shed the centers block and pushed him aside. And as Kevin back peddled, Randy rushed—letting out a loud yell.

"Ahhhhhhhhhhhhhhh," he screamed.

Forced out of the pocket, with one eye on Randy and another downfield, Kevin relied on his foot speed and sprinted to the right sideline. Randy was in hot pursuit, and Kevin was his prey.

Downfield, three receivers cris-crossed in an attempt to lose their defenders.

So far, it hadn't worked.

And as Kevin desperately looked for someone to throw to, Randy closed in. The earth seemed to quake beneath his feet.

Coming up from his safety position, another defender converged on Kevin too. His name was Larry, a well- built muscular boy, with an olive complexion. His eyes were dark brown. His hair was shiny black.

Kevin was about to become a sandwich, and he knew it. With no time to think, his instincts took over. Suddenly, he put on the brakes and stopped on a dime. And as Randy and Larry lunged, Kevin ducked.

Caught off guard, and unable to stop their momentum, the two defenders bodies collided with a loud thud. The air was filled with a mixture of sweat and spit. Like bugs hitting a windshield, Kevin was showered with the spray. The collision had been bone-jarring.

With no one left to chase him, and his foes entangled on the ground, Kevin calmly reversed his direction and looked downfield. He then hurled a high arcing pass to a wide-open receiver. His name was Paul. He was standing alone in an imaginary end zone between two large trees.

As Paul caught the pass, Kevin stretched his arms wide and high in triumph. "Yeah! Touchdown!"

Back lying on the ground, Randy and Larry looked at each other. Larry's jaw ached. He rubbed it. Laying next to him on the grass, Randy raised himself to his elbows. A wet substance was flowing from his pugged nose. He reached up and wiped it. It was only snot. Larry did the same. He found a little blood.

In the end zone, Paul was jumping up and down, shouting with glee. And as Kevin and his teammates trotted to him to congratulate him, Randy and Larry slowly got up. Joining their mates, they began the long walk to the other end of the field.

Like so many times before, Kevin Campbell had managed to pull off the clutch play. A fact Randy Milligan was all too familiar with as Kevin turned and yelled out after him.

"Suckers walk the field!" Kevin goaded.

Randy wasn't amused.

He shoved his hand into the air, "Ahh, shut up, Campbell!"

Arriving home from work, Bill, hot and dirty from a day spent on the "tanks," got out of his truck and walked to the front door. Entering the kitchen, he set his lunch pail down on the kitchen table.

In the living room, sitting on the floor was Rebecca, age four. She was blonde-haired, blue-eyed, and cute as a button. Bill glanced over at her and smiled. She was watching an episode of *Rocky and Bullwinkle* on the television. She turned her head briefly and flashed a smile at Bill.

"Hello daddy," she said before she looked back at the TV.

"Hello pumpkin," Bill replied.

"I don't know Rocky, sounds dangerous to me," Bullwinkle said from the TV.

Bill yelled to the back bedroom.

"Mary! I'm home. Did you get the mail?"

A faint voice replied. "Just a minute honey, I'll be out in a second."

Looking around, Bill spotted what he was looking for. It was sitting on the counter top. He reached over and grabbed it, then sat down.

As Bill rifled through the stack of mail, he came upon a white legal-sized envelope addressed to him. The return address said it was from P.A.L.—The Police Athletic League. Bill hastily ripped it open and pulled out the contents. As he did, Mary Campbell, a petite woman, age of 35, entered the room.

She was wiping her hands with a towel. Her short brown hair was curled on the sides. Her blue eyes twinkled as she spoke.

"I see you found it," she said.

Bill nodded as he read to himself silently. Mary pulled out a chair, and sat down beside him.

"Well?" she asked. Bill's eyes and lips moved as he read. He quickly looked up, cocked his head and smiled.

"We got our team," he announced.

"Really?" Mary said, with excitement in her voice.

"Yep," Bill replied as he continued to read.

"Well, what does it say?" Mary asked impatiently.

Bill quickly finished the letter, and held it out for her to read. She took it from his hand.

On the kitchen wall beside Bill was a calendar. He leaned back in his chair, and looked at it. It said August, 1964. Bill studied it for a moment, as Mary began to read the letter out loud.

"Dear Mr. Campbell, this letter is in response to your recent petition requesting entrance into this year's fifth- and sixth-grade city league. We are pleased to inform you your petition has been granted."

Mary continued to read to herself softly, as Bill looked through the rest of the mail. As she finished, Bill looked up at her.

"The season starts in less than three weeks," he said. "I better get a hold of Dale. We got a lot of work to do."

Mary nodded. She looked a little surprised. Something in the letter caught her eye.

"I see they gave you Carver too," she said.

"Yeah, how 'bout that," Bill replied.

Not far from the Campbell house, Kevin, Randy, Larry and Paul had finished their sandlot game. All four boys were on their bicycles. Two by two, hot and sweaty, they crossed a busy street. Once on the other side, they each jumped the curb and rode their bikes onto the sidewalk.

Under Kevin's arm was his football, neatly tucked.

Up ahead about a half of a block, was City Hall—a large, gray, concrete building. As they arrived at the front steps, each boy ditched his bike, and raced for the door.

In a long hallway the boys noisily made their entrance. Kevin was in the lead. Making his way to a water fountain, Kevin arrived first, and began to drink heavily. Randy was next in line. He looked thirsty.

"Hurry up, will ya!" he impatiently chided.

Kevin finally gave in and wiped his mouth. As he did, Randy bent over and placed his entire mouth over the fountainhead and began to drink heavily. Behind him, Larry looked repulsed.

"Ah man, ya got your mouth all over it!" he complained.

Paul agreed. "That's disgusting!"

And as Randy finished and caught up with Kevin, Larry wiped the fountainhead with his shirt and mumbled, "What a slob."

Down the hall, Kevin and Randy approached a large glass trophy case. Kevin stuck his nose against the glass and surveyed its contents.

Larry and Paul finally caught up. In the trophy case, one trophy among many others had their attention. It said *State Champions, Central High School 1948*. Next to it was a plaque with the names of about 40 team members. Kevin scanned it carefully.

"See! There it is. I told ya! Bill Campbell." On the plaque, was his father's name, and beside it was Darrell Phipps.

On the other side of the trophy case was a championship trophy for fifth- and sixth- grade city league. The boys slid their faces across the glass to look at it.

All of the past winners were etched into the brass plate. The last four years showed the dominance of the McKinley Knights: 1960 McKinley Knights, 1961 McKinley Knights, 1962 McKinley Knights, 1963 McKinley Knights, 1964 was still blank.

Randy was more than impressed. "Man, McKinley practically owns that thing," he said.

But Kevin was undaunted. "Yeah, well it's gonna say Adams after this year."

The rest of the boys looked at Kevin like he was crazy.

"Well it is," Kevin insisted.

Next to the trophy was a plaque titled "MVP City League: Fifth & Sixth Grade." There were many names on it, but the past four winners were all McKinley Knights, including Brad Phipps in 1963. The 1964 space was still blank.

Kevin pointed at it.

"And that one's gonna have my name on it."

Randy had heard enough, and he gave Kevin a shove.

"Ahhh, shut up Campbell!"

A little later that afternoon, as Kevin and his friends rode their bicycles home, Kevin thought about many things—of his father, and football, and of the season that was to be. He dreamed of winning that championship trophy, and of seeing his name on the plaque beside it.

What Kevin could never have dreamed of, was what actually happened over the course of the next several weeks.

No, not in a million years.

CHAPTER TWO

With less than three weeks before the start of the Pee Wee football season, Bill knew he had a lot of work to do. To start with, they would need a sponsor. New equipment was not cheap. And without a sponsorship, it would be nearly impossible to fully equip his new team. But if worse came to worse, Bill had already decided to pay for the equipment himself. All told, he would need a sum of about $300, an equivalent of about 3 weeks of his pay.

The following day, with the oil storage tanks of Champlin refinery shining brightly in the early morning sun, Bill entered Gate 5, with only one thing on his mind—to find a sponsor.

It wasn't until noon when Bill got his first real chance to sit down and talk with Dale Edwards. Dale was Bill's best friend. Standing about six feet tall with a medium build, Dale was a tough, hard working no nonsense man. He and Bill had been best friends for nearly 20 years. They had gone to high school together. They had played football together, and at times had been inseparable. For the past two years, Dale had also been Bill's assistant coach.

During a quick phone call the night before, Bill had spoken with Dale briefly about their acceptance into the city league.

Bill was eager to get Dale's input. As of yet they had not discussed the most interesting development—the fact that the city league had also given them Carver Elementary—the only black public elementary school in town.

Although Bill had only requested permission to form a team from the Adam's school district, the league, in their wisdom, saw fit to give him Carver as well. For Bill, the thought of an additional pool of kids to choose from had some appeal.

But this was 1964, and nobody in this town had ever integrated black kids before. Bill wasn't entirely sure he wanted to be the first.

So, inside the break room that day as they ate lunch, Bill Campbell discussed the letter with Dale. As they talked, Bill pulled out a pen from the pocket of his blue cotton buttoned-down shirt, and began to write on a napkin what he felt to be their most pressing needs.

Seated next them that afternoon was Roger Hayes, a heavy- set man, co-worker and friend. The three men were not alone. All around the room at various tables were other men, eating their lunches and carrying on conversations.

As Roger read the acceptance letter, Bill finished jotting down his thoughts. Roger immediately picked up on the last few lines of the letter.

"I see they threw in Colored Town," he chuckled. "A lot of good that'll do ya!"

Dale shook his head and grinned. "Yeah, really."

Bill had other concerns. He tapped at his napkin with his pen. "What we need is a sponsor," he said.

Dale leaned back in his chair and tossed in his two cents, "Have you talked to Ed yet? Maybe the union will sponsor us?"

Bill immediately winced, "Are you kidding? Since when has Ed Rivers ever done anything for us?"

Bill's reply apparently touched a nerve, and Dale let him know about it.

"Hey, It was just a thought!" Dale said as he tussled his short brown hair. Bill shook his head.

"Couldn't hurt to ask?" Roger added.

After few moments, Dale got up from the table and tossed his trash into the can. As he and Bill went back to work that afternoon, Bill pondered Dale's suggestion.

It wasn't that Bill had intended to offend his friend. In fact, he valued his advice greatly. However, based upon his past experience, getting the union to sponsor anything was not an easy task.

He tried to get them to sponsor his third- and fourth- grade team, to no avail. It was something that bothered him to this day.

As Bill always said, it seemed "Union sponsorships were only reserved for the brothers, uncles, nephews, and cousins of the local union rep. If you weren't related, you didn't get one."

In the end, last year, they settled for some left over equipment from a defunct team. Needless to say, the equipment wasn't in the best shape. This year, Bill had vowed he would do better.

As Bill went back to work that afternoon, he started to think Dale's suggestion might not have been such a bad one after all. And as the high-pitched steam whistle blew over the refinery, and he and his fellow co-workers lined up to leave work, Bill decided to give Ed another try.

As he ascended the flight of stairs leading to the Union rep's office, Bill rehearsed what he would say. Ed was a small burly man, and was well known as a tough negotiator. That's why he had the job.

Bill knew it would take some persuading. When the time came, and Ed returned to his desk, Bill was ready—and gave him his best pitch.

That afternoon, Bill tried everything to get Ed to commit. At first, Ed sat stone-faced as he listened to Bill's plea. But as the conversation wore on, Bill realized he wasn't getting anywhere. It seemed as if Ed had already made up his mind.

Bill even pleaded to his sense of duty pointing out all of the union's other past sponsorships and awards represented on the wall behind Ed's desk—but nothing worked.

Outside the office, there were faint sounds of typewriters clicking. It was starting to get on Bill's nerves. So was Ed.

"Sorry Bill," Ed said, "You know I'd like to help ya, but we just can't afford to right now."

"That's all right Ed," Bill said. "I knew I was wastin' my time when I first came in here."

"Now wait a second, Bill, don't go off bein' mad at me. You know we'd like to help ya." Ed then leaned back in his chair, and added. "You know how tight money is around here."

Ed motioned to the same memorabilia Bill had pointed out behind him on the wall. "Besides that, I got everybody and their brothers' uncle tryin' to get me to sponsor 'em. I can't very well say yes to everyone."

Bill shook his head in frustration. "Yeah," Bill said. And with that, Bill decided to give in. He stood up with his hardhat and lunch pail in hand, and headed for the door.

Ed frowned a little. He looked repentant. "I tell you what Bill," he sighed. "I'll make you a deal?"

Bill exited the union office, and walked down the stairs. Outside the union office, near gate number five; Dale sat squatting on his lunch pail. By the way he was squirming on his improvised seat, he had no doubt been waiting for quite a while.

Upon seeing Bill, Dale quickly jumped to his feet and anxiously waited for his friend. As Bill negotiated the steel steps, and walked down the long narrow pathway to exit the refinery complex, Dale studied his face for a hint of news. As Bill walked past the guard and exited the gate with his steel hat and lunch pail in hand, Dale could tell that the news had not been good. He asked anyway.

"Well, What'd he say?" Dale asked.

Bill just shook his head. Dale's countenance fell.

"Why that cheap little—see if I ever pay my dues again." But no sooner had Dale vented his anger, Bill smiled, and Dale knew he'd been had.

"You got it, didn't ya?"

Bill smiled, "Yep."

Dale almost jumped into the air. He let out a small yell, "Yeeahh!" His voiced echoed as he hollered, *"Yesssss!"*

With the union sponsorship taken care of, Bill and Dale could now focus on forming a team—something they both looked forward to.

Last year's team had been a success. They had finished the season at 5-2. They made third place. This year they hoped to do better.

For the moment, one question still had the best of Dale. *How in the world had Bill gotten Ed to commit to such a large sponsorship?* As they walked on to their trucks, Dale decided to ask.

"How'd ya get him to do it anyway?"

"It was easy," Bill said. "Once I promised him we'd win the championship," Bill added.

Dale asked the obvious, "But what if we don't?"

Bill dropped the bombshell. "Well," he hesitated. "I told him you and I would personally pay the union back."

Dale's mouth nearly dropped to the ground. He couldn't believe Bill had made such a promise. After all, he considered himself to be a poor man.

That evening as the Campbell's sat down to supper, Bill told Mary all about his day. Everything, that is, except for the little side agreement he had made with Ed Rivers. It wasn't until after dinner, when Bill decided to fill Mary in about the sponsorship.

As Bill cleared the supper table, Mary ran some water in the sink, and prepared to do the dishes. Bill handed her a stack of plates.

"I got some good news today." Bill said. Mary added some dish washing liquid to the running water.

"Oh yeah, what's that?"

"The union agreed to sponsor the team this year."

Mary looked back at Bill, surprised. "Really?"

Bill nodded. "Yeah, they're gonna pay for uniforms and everything. They even agreed to keep me on day shift until the season's over."

Bill handed her another plate.

"How much are they givin' ya?" Mary inquired.

Bill walked back to the table, "About $300," he said nonchalantly.

Mary turned around to Bill. She looked skeptical. "And they're just gonna give it to ya?"

Bill nodded coolly and began gathering up the silverware. "Yeah. Well, kinda," he said.

Mary put her soapy hands against her hips. "What do you mean, *kinda*?" she said with a raised voice.

Bill seemed a little pensive as he handed her a pile of silverware. "Well, there is a slight chance we might have to pay it back."

Mary looked incredulous, "Three hundred dollars?"

Bill sheepishly nodded. Mary's mouth dropped open. "*Bill Campbell*! How could you go and do something like that?"

Bill looked contrite. "Well..."

Mary cut him off. "Where are we gonna get $300? You barely make that much in a month."

Bill carefully handed her the last of the tableware. Mary turned back to the sink and plunged them into the soapy water. He lowered his head a little, and carefully stepped toward her.

"Look, I know it's a lot of money, but it's not every day that I get a chance to coach Kevin." Bill reached around her waist and handed her a bowl. "Anyways, we might not have to pay it back."

Mary looked over her shoulder at Bill and raised her eyebrows. She then turned back to the sink.

Bill inched closer, put his arms around her waist and snuggled against her. "I had to take the deal honey, or we wouldn't have gotten anything." Bill nuzzled his nose against the side of her neck. "Besides, everyone else in town has got good equipment, why shouldn't we?"

Mary seemed to soften a little but remained unenthusiastic.

"*We're* not everyone else," she said.

Bill gently smooched on her neck. "You got that right," he said softly in between two tender kisses. Mary sighed as she bowed her neck and accepted his affection.

"Do you need help with the jerseys?" she asked.

Bill smiled, "Yeah, if you could."

Mary sighed, and smiled a little too. "I'll get a hold of Becky Edwards in the mornin', and we'll get started on 'em."

Thus, it was official. With Mom's stamp of approval, we became the United Oil Workers Union Oilers.

The following afternoon Mary, Becky Edwards, and a handful of women gathered in Mary's living room, and began the process of sewing gold letters and numbers onto black jerseys supplied by the local union. Mary seemed proud of her work, as she held up one of the finished jerseys and showed it to Becky.

Back at the refinery that same afternoon, Bill and Dale met once again in the break room. Roger joined them. There remained much work to be done. As the three men drank coffee and discussed the prospects for the new season, Bill pulled out a napkin and pen and point-by-point made his case on how they should proceed.

"Now look," he said, "we can put Eddie Griffin at fullback, Kevin can be quarterback, all we need is a good tailback, and we'll be all set."

But for Dale, it wasn't quite that simple—and it was obvious that something was troubling him. He had apparently heard some news Bill had not been privy to, and he finally got to the point.

"Look, we're gonna need more than a good offense if we wanna win this year. I heard Ted Cummings says Darrell Phipps is expecting 60 kids to come out."

Bill couldn't believe it could be true, but Dale insisted,

"That's what he said."

It was at this point that Roger jumped in, and made things worse. "I wouldn't doubt it. That district has got a lot of kids in it, I think they had nearly 50 kids out last year."

By this time Dale's concern had turned to a whine, "We'll be lucky if we get 25."

But Bill pointed out the fact they only needed 18 to form the team. That was the league mandate. By this time Dale's attitude had turned from bad to worse.

It seemed that the only thing he was concerned about was the $300 he and Bill had "borrowed" from the union. Bill said he didn't quite think of it as a "loan,"—but rather as a "commitment."

Roger sensing Dale was worried about the sponsorship money, decided to pour it on.

"All I know is you guys got your work cut out for ya. McKinley hasn't lost a championship in years."

Bill tried to intervene, "We almost beat 'em last year."

Roger persisted, "Yeah, well, that was their third- and fourth- grade team. This is different. I'm tellin' ya, they put 'em out like a factory."

With that, Roger leaned forward, and dumped the whole load on Dale. "And Darrell Phipps doesn't like to lose, if you know what I mean." He leaned back, "Nobody even came close to 'em last year."

Dale's face immediately went completely pale. Bill tried to revive him.

"Yeah, well, they put their pads on just like our kids do."

Roger was relentless. "Yeah, but they sure are *big* pads. Why half those kids looked like they belonged in junior high, not grade school."

By now Dale was starting to look a little mad. He tapped his fingers on the edge of the table and looked at Bill and gave him that "You're gonna pay for this" look.

Bill just shook his head and tried to blow it off.

Outside, the whistle finally blew, signaling the end of the break. Bill looked relieved to hear it. Roger smiled broadly and got up to go back to work. Bill and Dale did the same, except for the smiling.

CHAPTER THREE

If Dale's confidence was a little low, then Darrell Phipps was sky high. For on a grass field adjacent to McKinley Elementary, about 50 boys aged ten to twelve, all Caucasian, stood facing three coaches.

The largest of the three coaches was Darrell.

Standing six foot-two, weighing a solid 220 pounds, Darrell brimmed with confidence as he looked over his prospective team. He was well dressed in slacks and a sport shirt.

As he prepared to address his potential players, Darrell looked at one of the boys and softly winked. It was his son Brad. Brad was his spitting image. He was a good-sized boy, standing about 5 foot four, with blue eyes, and short brown hair.

Nearby, coach Baker, one of Darrell's numerous assistants, began to get a head count. Darrell watched, and then began to pace back and forth as he collected his thoughts.

After a few moments, he looked at Coach Baker. Coach Baker was finishing his count.

Baker paused and looked at Darrell, "Fifty-two, I think," he said. Darrell nodded, took center stage, and began addressing the boys.

"Now I want to thank all of you for coming out. This looks like our biggest turnout ever." Darrell checked with Baker. Baker nodded in the affirmative. Darrell looked back at the boys, and continued. "Coach Baker tells me there are 52 of ya. Unfortunately, we can only keep 45. That's all we have equipment for."

A low murmur began to break out among the boys. The disparity between the athletes and the wanna-bees was obvious. The boys all seemed to be sizing each other up.

Darrell continued. "Now I know of at least six more kids that aren't here today, that are comin' out tomorrow. So that means we're gonna have to make some cuts. Tryouts will be at 3 o'clock."

As Darrell kicked at a clump of grass, the boys did the math, and by the looks on a few of their faces, some already knew their fate. Darrell continued.

"Now I promise you, I'll do my very best to take a good look at each and every one of ya. So put on your track shoes and come prepared! And we'll see who's got the right stuff to become a *Knight!*"

Darrell turned to Baker. "Do you have anything to add coach?

Baker stepped forward. "Yeah, we need to talk about physicals and releases."

And with that, Darrell passed the baton, "All right, right now I'm gonna turn it over to Coach Baker. He's gonna give you some important information, so listen up."

Darrell looked at Baker and nodded, "Coach, they're all yours."

Darrell stepped back and made way for coach Baker. As he did, he proudly looked over the assembly of boys, like a farmer looks over a bumper crop. There had always been plenty of room on his teams before, but this years turnout was unusually large, no doubt due to their past success.

The fact was, the McKinley Knights were the best Pee Wee football team in the city's history, and everyone loved a winner. And having won four consecutive city championships, it seemed each year more and more boys showed up to try out for a spot on his team.

The competition was fierce.

On the edge of the field that day, while Darrell was addressing the kids, a group of parents had been watching the meeting. As Darrell made way for Coach Baker, two of them broke away and began walking his direction.

One of the men was Frank Felcher, a black haired man, with dark eyes. The other was Jack Howard. Jack was a local business man with sandy colored hair and blue eyes. He stood about six feet tall. He was about the same height as Frank, but looked like he never missed a meal. He was a bit pudgy around the waist.

As Darrell noticed the two men walking his way, his eyes lit up. Darrell met them half way. As the men approached, Frank smiled and extended his hand.

"How ya doin' coach?"

Darrell reciprocated, "Good Frank, how 'bout yourself?"

Frank nodded, and the two men shook.

"Jack, good to see ya." Darrell loosed his grip and shook Jack's hand, and then turned back to Frank. "Looks like Lance put on a little weight."

Across the field, the men glanced over at a well-built boy. It was Frank's son—his spitting image.

Frank looked proud, "Yeah, he's been workin' hard all summer."

Jack jumped in, "What kind of team are we gonna have this year coach?"

Darrell looked confident, "Looks like it might be our best one yet."

Frank was genuinely happy, "Good! Who's our competition, any idea?" Darrell thought about it for a moment, folded his arms, and then pushed out his lower lip.

"Pretty much the same as last year, the Vikings are always tough. Other than that, I don't see anyone sneakin' up on us." Then he added,

"There is one new team though."

"Oh yeah, who's that," Jack asked.

"Adams Elementary, Bill Campbell is the coach."

Scott Staerkel

Frank and Jack looked at each other, and then shook their heads. Neither of the men had ever heard of Bill Campbell, and Darrell didn't act too concerned.

"It ain't no big deal. I went to high school with Bill. We played ball together. Nice guy. Average player. We'll kick their butts."

Meanwhile, back on the east side of town, on the grassy field next to the playground of Adams Elementary, Bill and Dale were scratching their heads trying to figure out what had just happened. For while Darrell and his assistants were preparing to toss back players like a fisherman over his limit, Bill and Dale had no such luck. Only fifteen boys showed up—not even enough to make a team.

The boys were facing Bill and Dale. Bill looked at his watch once more, and then scanned the horizon. It was 4:30, and they were three kids short of an official team.

About half of the boys were from the earlier sandlot game, they were all wearing street clothes. Off to the side were several tall boxes full of equipment, brand- spanking new— compliments of the local union.

Bill looked at the boxes and shook his head. *"Well,"* he thought, *"at least the sponsorship came through."*

Not far away, a handful of parents, including Joe Carter, a short, stocky man with huge forearms, stood at a distance and watched. Bill looked over at the parents, and then back at the boys.

He still could not believe his eyes. He turned to Dale, "This can't be all the kids?"

Dale shook his head and confirmed the obvious. "That must be it."

Bill frowned. "Why last year we had twice as many." He then added, "Randy, Paul and Kevin can't be the only fifth graders?"

Dale shrugged. Bill stepped toward the boys.

"All right, before we pass out the equipment, there are a few things we need to talk about. First, we need some more kids. We gotta have at least 18 if we're gonna field a team. That's the rule.

"Now I don't know what happened, but a lot of your buddies didn't show up today. So get the word out, tell 'em to come on out, it's not too late. Otherwise we won't have a team."

The boys looked a little worried. They could tell Bill was serious.

Bill continued. "Second, our first game is in less than three weeks, and we've got a lot of work to do. I want you to start studying these play sheets that I am about to give ya."

Bill reached over, took a handful of play sheets from Dale, and held them up. "By next week, I'll expect you to know 'em. Most of you already know your positions—but if you don't, don't worry about it—we'll take care of that tomorrow."

Bill handed the sheets to Kevin. Kevin began handing them out.

As Kevin passed out the sheets of paper, Bill paced back and forth in front of the boys. As he paced, he attempted to collect his thoughts. Inside, his stomach was churning like crazy.

Standing nearby, Dale bit his fingernails, and stared off into the distance. He looked concerned too. Suddenly, Dale remembered the release forms he was holding in his other hand, and he extended them toward Bill.

Bill reached over and took them, "Oh yeah, and I almost forgot," Bill added. "This release form *has got* to be filled out. You can't play football in the city league until you've turned one of these in. So take it home and get it signed—*tonight*. Bring it back tomorrow when we start practice. If you don't, you can't play. Is that understood?"

The boys all nodded. Bill looked at Dale. "Do you have anything else to add?"

Dale shook his head, and walked toward the boxes containing their new equipment.

Bill clapped his hands together and motioned for the boys, "All right, form a single file line right over here."

As Bill and Dale passed out the equipment that afternoon, Bill was worried sick. Everyone knew today was the official sign-up day for the new season. It had been well publicized.

Last year 24 kids showed up on the first day, and then no more. They'd had more than enough to field a team. Bill was very concerned. Dale was too, but reasoned with Bill that more would likely show up.

"Some kids were bound to still be on vacation," Dale said.

But Bill wasn't so sure, and as he and Dale finished passing out the equipment that afternoon, Bill had a bad feeling in he pit of his stomach. In his mind, this was absolutely the worst thing that could happen. He had never dreamed they would have trouble getting enough kids.

Later that evening, as Bill and Kevin drove home from the practice field with the boxes of left over equipment stacked neatly in the back of their truck, Bill went over and over last year's roster in his mind.

Where was Tommy Franklin, and little David Elder? he wondered. *And where were all the other boys who were members of last years team?*

As they drove down Market Street toward home, Kevin could see the concern etched on his father's face.

Up ahead was Sixth Street. And off to the right, down about a half block was a set of railroad tracks. Kevin looked out his window at them. Across the tracks was the beginning of a very poor neighborhood.

As Bill approached the intersection, the light turned yellow and then red. Bill coasted his truck to a stop.

If you asked anyone—what was to the south of the intersection of Market and Sixth, they would tell you it was "Colored Town." Dubbed "The Ville" by local residents, "Colored Town" was an all- too- familiar sight to Bill. He lived just six blocks away, and had driven by it at least a thousand times.

That evening, as he and Kevin were stopped at the red light, he looked off to the right past the railroad tracks at an adjacent vacant lot. Nothing seemed out of the ordinary. Except for the fact several black boys were playing football.

The ball they were using was bloated, and ripped at the seam. The light, as Bill would later recall, was long and red. And but for a brief moment, his attention had been riveted on one of the boys. He watched in amazement as the kid received a kick, and gracefully eluded at least a half a dozen tacklers. He was using moves Bill had never seen before.

There, in that vacant lot, was the obvious solution to Bill Campbell's player shortage. But instead of making the immediate connection, his thoughts were elsewhere. As the light turned green, Bill was still watching the boy run. Behind him, an anxious driver honked his horn. The sound of it startled Bill back reality. He looked in his rear view mirror at the impatient motorist. Being reminded of where he was, Bill stepped on the gas, and headed home.

CHAPTER FOUR

If there were a shortage of eleven- and twelve- year-olds in this small town, you wouldn't have known it by the turnout at McKinley Elementary.

The city was growing west. With it went most of the town's money and influence. McKinley was a prime benefactor. Its enrollment had increased every year—and that meant more tax dollars. As a consequence, McKinley was by far and away the best- equipped and staffed school in the area.

In contrast, Adams, and those who attended the schools located on the east side of town, were relatively poor. Some people had good jobs, like Bill and Dale. But on the whole, the incomes of the east- side residents were far less than the better-educated—and more affluent citizens—who all seemed to migrate west.

And then there was Colored Town. That small section of town on the southeast side—a place far removed from the population at large. A place where white folks rarely ventured, let alone spent their tax dollars.

As the early evening sun shone brightly across the well-manicured grass field adjacent to Mckinley, Darrell and his three assistants were hard at work conducting tryouts. Darrell's early estimate was no exaggeration. 58 boys had showed up, all shapes and sizes, all Caucasian.

Having neatly formed two lines, the boys were waiting to be timed. At the opposite end of the field, Darrell stood holding a stopwatch. Next to him was Coach Baker. He had a clipboard in hand.

As Darrell blew his whistle for the umteenth time that afternoon, another boy took off running at him. About six seconds later, as the boy crossed the line; Darrell clicked his stopwatch, and then leaned over to Baker. "Too slow," Darrell said.

Baker nodded and scratched the boy's name off the list.

Darrell looked at the boy and patronized him. "Good run son."

The boy smiled, then trotted back to the other end of the field. Darrell blew his whistle again, and another boy took off. As he began running, his sides shook like a barrel full of jelly.

Darrell squinted his eyes, and then with disgust in his voice declared his thoughts, "Too fat."

Once again, Baker nodded and crossed his name off the list. It seemed like an eternity to Darrell, but the boy finally crossed the line.

As he did, Darrell greeted him in a cheerful, but sarcastic tone, "Good effort!"

Darrell then blew his whistle once more, and another boy took off. Clicking his watch as he crossed the line, Darrell looked at Baker and shook his head. He muttered in a low voice, "Too small."

Baker leaned toward him. "His dad is one of our sponsors."

Darrell acted like he'd seen the light, "Shooo, you're right, I forgot about that."

And with that, Baker put a check beside the boy's name. And as the boy crossed back in front of him, Darrell looked impressed, "Good job, son!" He then looked over at Baker. "How many more do we need to cut?"

Baker scanned his clipboard, "Six."

Darrell blew his whistle once again.

On the other end of the field, another boy sprinted at them. As he did, Darrell philosophized, "You know what I like best about coachin'?"

Baker scanned his clipboard, then looked up at Darrell. "What's that?"

Darrell appeared to be lost in another world. "You get to make the little buggers do what ever you want 'em to, and they gotta love it!"

As the boy crossed the line, he sprinted past them about 15 yards. As Darrell came back to reality, he raised the stopwatch from his side, and looked at it. He had forgot to time him, but apparently, it didn't matter.

Darrell continued to reflect, "Remember how you used to have to do all those drills and then run 'til your tongue fell out after practice? I always wondered what it would be like to be on the other side."

As the boy crossed back in front of him, Darrell looked at the watch again, and then back at the boy.

"Good time, son!"

The boy looked hopeful. Darrell waited until his back was turned, and shook his head. Baker scratched his name off the list.

Darrell sighed. He looked impatient. "How many more?"

Baker scanned his clipboard. "Five."

While Darrell was cutting a dozen or so kids from his roster, Bill Campbell was still looking for a few more to fill out his. The first official practice of the season had not yielded any more boys.

It was a fact, that weighed heavily upon Bill's mind as he sat down to eat his evening meal. His dream of fielding a competitive team now seemed unattainable. Even though Carver had been assigned to his district, he knew all too well, there would be opposition if he dared go over there.

Bill was a practical man. A practical man would look elsewhere, first.

There was almost an eerie silence at the supper table that evening as the Campbell's ate supper. The pressure was on

Bill. Dale had already said he didn't want anything to do with Colored Town, and Bill was having a hard time enjoying his evening meal.

Kevin had no such trouble, it seemed he couldn't keep his fork going fast enough. Bill gestured to him from across the table. "Slow down will ya, your gonna make yourself sick."

Kevin slowed down momentarily, as Mary took a sip from her glass of water and then broke her silence.

"How was practice today?"

Bill dug at his plate, "All right."

Mary persisted. "Any more boys come out?"

Bill swallowed and ran his tongue across his teeth, "Nope."

But Mary wouldn't let him off that easy. "There's gotta be some more around somewhere?"

Bill remained coy, "Yep."

Mary couldn't contain it anymore. "Well, why don't you go get 'em?"

Kevin looked at his father like, *Yeah. Why don't ya?* Bill looked back at Kevin like *give me a break will ya?*

The following day after practice, Bill and Dale decided to hit the streets. It had been a long, hot day at the refinery, and even at 6 p.m. the heat seemed unrelenting. Sun- drenched and sweat- soaked, the two men pounded on every door.

Most residents would only shake their heads, a few would point down the street, but over and over again, the result was the same. There were no more boys. Finally, Dale said he'd had enough and suggested they go home. Bill agreed, and the two men parted the same way they came, empty-handed.

That evening as Bill took off his work boots and stretched out in his easy chair, his mind began to race. He looked hot and tired. He was sweating profusely. Mary was standing behind him, trying to comfort him by rubbing his shoulders.

In front of him, on the Campbell's black and white television set was news footage of a plantation owner in Mississippi talking to a reporter about the voter registration drive.

The volume was down low.

"If any of my niggers try to register, I'll shoot them down like rabbits," the plantation owner said.

But Bill wasn't paying attention to the TV, and Mary wasn't either.

"Did you try *every* house," Mary asked?

"Honey we went to every house, from here to Market Street, if there was a male child born after '52, we'd a known it."

Mary sighed. "Well, what happened to everyone anyway?"

Bill shook his head. "Well, Tommy Franklin's dad got transferred to Omaha, so he's gone. David Elder moved to the west side, Les Akins broke his leg, and I don't know about the rest of 'em."

"Have you tried Carver yet," Mary asked?

Bill shook his head; his eyes were searching. "I don't know why I started this team in the first place," Bill lamented.

But Mary knew why, and she reminded him. "Kevin," she said softly.

Bill was lost in thoughts. "Huh?" he asked.

"You started it for Kevin," Mary said.

"Yeah," Bill replied.

Mary shook her head, "Oh well there is always next year."

But Bill was resolute. "No there ain't, there is only now."

The following day, 15 solitary players lined up to receive their brand- new game jerseys. Appropriately, Bill had chosen the color of "off black" with gold numbers. Being the coach's son, Kevin had gotten first pick of the numbers, and chose eleven.

Unfortunately, there were still plenty of numbers to pick from. Each jersey sported the United Oil Workers Union logo on the shoulder with the name "OILERS" spread out across the chest.

Bill looked proud as he watched each boy put on his new jersey. Nevertheless, he couldn't help but think this might be just a waste of time.

On Saturday morning, a chill in the air greeted Bill as he woke up. It was a reminder September was less than a week away, and with it was the deadline for turning in the official team roster.

But today there was other work to be done. That afternoon, Bill had promised Kevin he would take him downtown to look at a letter jacket. The coolness of the air now reminded him of it. So after a morning of "honey do's", Bill and Kevin hopped in the truck and drove downtown.

Even though the city had a growing population of about 30,000, it was not uncommon to run into someone that you knew. So as Bill and Kevin walked along a downtown sidewalk that afternoon, it wasn't much of a surprise as to how many acquaintances they bumped into. What was a surprise, was *who*.

Approaching Bill and Kevin from the other end of the sidewalk was Darrell, well- dressed and brimming with confidence. Walking beside him was his twelve-year-old son Brad. Brad was also dressed for the day wearing a blue letter jacket with a large Letter M on the left side of his chest.

On each of his shoulders were several patches, shaped like footballs, reflecting championships, and All- Star teams. The jacket was very similar to the one Kevin had his eye on, except for the color.

As Bill made eye contact with the Phipps, his face stiffened. This was the last person he wanted to run into today. Darrell's reaction was quite the opposite. His eyes lit up as he saw Bill.

As the two men approached each other, Darrell extended his hand, "Bill Campbell! How the hell are ya! I haven't seen you in—must be—six months."

"It's been awhile," Bill replied.

Darrell probed, "Yeah, well, how ya been?"

Bill seemed defensive, "Good, workin' hard as usual."

Darrell dug at him. "How's that new team comin'?"

Bill thought for a moment, then looked him in the eye and lied, "Good!"

Darrell knew better. "Is that right? I heard ya was havin' trouble findin' enough kids?"

Bill put his arm around Kevin's shoulder as if to gain support, "Oh no, we got enough."

Kevin immediately looked up at his father like *what are you talking about?* Bill tightened his grip on Kevin. Kevin seemed to have gotten his message, and straightened up. Darrell pulled his son to himself, and raised the stakes.

"Yeah well, we had 58 come out this year, best group yet."

Bill tried to act like it was news. "Really? You all will probably have a pretty good team then?"

Darrell smiled smugly, "The usual."

At this point, Bill wanted out of the conversation in the worst way. So he stepped to the side, and extended his hand, "Well hey, it's been nice seein' ya."

Darrell nodded, and shook his hand, "Yeah, you too."

As Bill and Kevin began to move on. Darrell and Brad did the same. As Kevin and Bill walked down the sidewalk, Kevin was smiling from ear to ear.

Bill looked down at him and asked, "What are you smilin' at?"

Kevin looked up at his father, and replied, "You lied to him. Didn't ya?"

Bill looked back over his shoulder at the Phipps with a glint in his eye, "Yeah, I reckon I did."

With a weekend of rest behind him, Bill felt much better. By Monday afternoon he was ready to get back to practice. By all accounts, the practice went well—or at least Bill thought so. They had already put in most of their offense, and their defense was in pretty good shape. Most of the boys were playing both ways.

But as the practice concluded that Monday afternoon, Bill had other things on his mind. They still needed the three boys to field an official team, and Bill knew where to get them.

As he and Dale gathered up the practice dummies, and tossed them into the back of Bill's truck, Bill decided to make his case.

"You're gonna do what?" Dale responded.

Bill threw one of the dummies into the bed of the truck. "I said," Bill reiterated, "I think I'm gonna go look for those colored boys I saw the other day, and ask 'em if they want to play."

Dale was a bit taken back. "I don't know Bill. We may be short, but we're not *that* desperate."

But Bill was, and it showed in his voice. "We need more kids, don't we?"

Dale hedged, "Yeah, but —"

Bill picked up another dummy, tossed it into the bed of the truck and fired back, "But *what*?"

Dale was starting to think he was serious. He laughed uncomfortably.

"I don't know if that's such a good idea?"

Bill was serious, and put it to him. "You got a better one?"

Dale thought for a moment, but didn't respond.

Bill continued, "Look, they're a part of our district, and besides, there's one boy who looked like he'd be awful good."

Bill then picked up the last dummy and threw it into the back of his truck. He walked to the driver's side door and looked back at Dale, "You comin' or not?"

Dale exhaled and reluctantly nodded, "I guess it wouldn't hurt to just *look*."

A few minutes later Bill and Dale drove by the vacant lot where Bill had seen the boys playing football. They were not there. Bill stopped at the light, and then suddenly turned left. They were headed right into the middle of Colored Town.

Dale was shocked, "Where are you going?" he asked.

Bill pushed the accelerator to the floor, and shifted gears. "To find those boys," he replied.

Dale looked incredulous, "I thought we were just gonna *look*, we can't actually go *in* there!"

Bill kept driving. "Why not?"

Dale was beside himself. *"Why not?"*

By this time, Bill and Dale had already traveled a few blocks. The neighborhoods were clean and neat—but very poor. Dale slumped down in his seat as Bill surveyed the area. The two white men were beginning to stick out like sore thumbs.

Their appearance had not escaped the notice of the black residents. Dale was very uncomfortable. Bill found a clear spot and pulled over to the curb.

As Bill opened his door and started to get out, Dale's nervousness increased. "Now what are you doing?"

Bill had had enough, "Relax, will ya? I'm just gonna ask if anyone has seen 'em."

Bill got out and shut the door. He looked back into the cab, and reassured Dale, "I'll only be a minute."

Dale shook his head. He didn't want to be there.

As Bill walked across the street, he decided to go a few houses down where an older gentleman was sitting on a porch. All around the neighborhood blacks were slowly appearing.

A few looked curious, some looked distrustful. Bill approached the front porch, and gestured to the man.

"How ya doin'?"

The man on the porch slowly responded. "All right."

Bill continued, "I noticed some boys playin' ball in that lot over there." Bill pointed at the vacant lot. "I was wonderin' if you know where I might be able to find them?"

The old man on the porch, looked toward the lot, and then back at Bill. "Somebody in trouble?"

Bill shook his head, "No, no, I'm a coach, football. Do ya know the boys I'm talkin' about?"

The man on the porch looked Bill in the eye. "A lotta boys play football around here," he said.

Bill nodded. "Any of 'em in the fifth or sixth grade?"

"I'm sure there are a few," the man responded. He stood up and pointed down the street. "You might have better luck down by the school. A lot of the kids like to hang out down there."

Bill acknowledged him, "I appreciate it." The old man nodded, and Bill walked back to the truck. As he opened the door and got in, Dale looked happy to see him. Bill started the truck, and drove down the street.

Upon arriving at his destination, Bill parked his truck across the street from Carver Elementary. The school was in obvious need of repair. Several of the windows were cracked, and the paint was peeling badly.

Walking across the street, Bill headed for the playground next to the school. Dale stayed behind, to—as he put it, "Watch the truck."

There were a few kids playing on the playground, but none were the right age. Bill looked at them. They seemed to ignore his presence. Putting his hands on his hips, Bill thought for a moment, and then decided to walk the block and canvass the neighborhood. One block became another. There were plenty of kids, but none of them seemed to be the right age.

Finally, Bill decided to give it up. The boys he was looking for were nowhere to be seen. As Bill walked back to the truck, not far from the school, a boy -about age 12—suddenly appeared from the side of a house.

He was running at a pretty good clip. A little girl, about age eight, was chasing him. The boy looked familiar, Bill thought.

Bill watched him run. It was *him*. It was the same boy that had caught his eye at the vacant lot. Caught up in the chase, and looking back over his shoulder, he nearly ran right over Bill.

With a surprised look on his face, he quickly apologized, "Oops! Sorry, mister."

The girl chasing him was giggling for all it was worth. The near collision, and apology, had caused him to slow down just enough for the girl to catch him.

And she did. "Gotcha Charles!"

But no sooner had she touched him, the little girl took off running the same way in which she came. Charles looked at Bill, and then took off after her.

"Why you little..." he said, mumbling.

Bill was caught off guard. He watched for a moment, and then realized the boy was getting away, and yelled out after him.

"Hey! Wait a minute!" But it was too late, Charles had disappeared.

Standing in disbelief that he'd let him get away, Bill put his hands on his waist and shook his head. After a moment, he walked back to the truck. He opened the door, and then looked back at where Charles had disappeared. The boy was nowhere in sight. In the cab, Dale was anxious; he leaned across the seat and looked up at Bill.

"Well that's that. Let's get out of here."

But Bill wasn't paying attention to Dale. He continued to look, and surveyed the area once more.

Inside the cab, Dale was getting impatient. "Look, we ain't supposed to be over here in the first place, so get in and start this thing—and let's get outta here."

Bill looked into the cab. Dale looked serious.

As Bill opened the door and got in, Dale gestured to the keys in the ignition. Bill shut the door, and put his hand on the keys.

"You are kidding aren't you?" Bill asked.

Dale shook his head emphatically, "Nope. Now start this thing, and let's go home."

48

Bill dropped his hand, and looked back at him like he was crazy. "Go home? If you haven't forgot, we got two days to get three kids or we ain't got a team!"

Dale looked back at him like *so what?* Bill was dumbfounded.

"Look Dale, we've been to every house in our district, and a few outside of it." Bill pointed to the ground. "Everywhere that is except for *here*. This ain't no time to be givin' up. If anything, we oughta be goin' door to door!"

But Dale wasn't buying it, "Not *me,* not *here!,* I'm goin' home." And with that, Dale pointed straight at him. "And you're gonna take me. Now get it in gear—and let's go."

Bill couldn't believe his ears. This was their last hope, and he knew it. But Dale looked resolute, so Bill clenched his teeth, started the truck, put it in gear, and sped off down the street.

That evening, as Bill drove Dale back to the practice field and let him off at his truck, Bill felt horrible. He and Dale hadn't said a word to each other the whole trip back. That night as he went to bed, Bill thought about his Oilers, and vowed to himself that somehow—some way—he would find enough players— even if he had to do it by himself.

CHAPTER FIVE

It was 5 a.m., the sound of the alarm clock on the night stand startled Bill from his sleep.

He had been dreaming. What about he wasn't exactly sure, but he wished it could have continued. He had barely slept.

Lying next to him, Mary was sound asleep. Bill glanced at her. In the moonlight, her face seemed to exude her natural warmth. *She was beautiful*, he thought. Bill reached out across her, and smothered the alarm clock to put an end to its ringing bell.

Lying back on his pillow, Bill looked up at the ceiling, and attempted to gather his thoughts. He looked across the room at an open window.

The heat of the night had given way to a soft, cool breeze. Mary breathed softly. The thin, white cotton curtain covering the window seemed to dance with her every breath.

As the cool breeze wafted over him, Bill mustered enough strength to raise himself up, put one foot on the floor, and then the other. Facing the window, he steadied himself on the edge of the bed.

It was time to get ready for work.

A few hours later, Bill sat alone at a table in the break room of the refinery. For the first time in a long time he felt alone. As he drank his coffee, his mind raced. Across from Bill that morning, at the other end of an adjoining table sat Dale. The argument the night before had put a momentary strain on their friendship. For now, the two men were not even speaking to each other. Neither one would make eye contact, even though they both had plenty of opportunity.

A few tables over, Roger and another co-worker were engaged in a long conversation. Seated around them at various tables were many of their fellow co-workers.

Some of them were also parents of the "Oilers," including Joe Carter—something Roger had said had obviously gotten Joe's attention. He looked rather attentive. After a moment, Joe stood up and walked over to Bill's table, grabbed the edge and leaned over toward Bill.

"Hey Bill," Joe said in a hushed tone. "What's this I hear that you and Dale paid a little visit to Colored Town last night?"

Bill looked at Dale as if he had been betrayed. Dale looked away. Bill looked up at Joe. "Yeah, so what?"

Joe looked angry. He inched closer. So close, Bill could smell the coffee on his breath. Joe raised his voice a little, "*So what?* What're ya doin' over there?"

"Lookin' for kids," Bill said.

Joe raised his voice another notch, "You mean *niggers.*"

Joe's comment had everyone's attention. The break room grew silent. It now seemed everyone in the room was a party to their conversation. Dale lowered his head. He knew what was coming. Bill squirmed in his chair, glanced over at Dale and then looked back up at Joe.

"Look Joe, we need more kids. I mean what's the big deal, they got 'em in the pros?"

Joe remained unconvinced. "Yeah, well this ain't the pros—and you ain't payin' anyone."

At an adjoining table another worker piped up. "Yeah, and next thing ya know, they'll be practicin' with hubcaps and watermelons."

The entire room erupted with laughter. Bill's face stiffened. He angrily shook his head.

Across the room, against the wall, another voice boomed out. It was another of the Oiler parents who had been attending the practices.

"Yeah Bill, what's goin' on? We ain't ever needed the colored's before?"

Bill pushed his chair back so that he could make eye contact with the faceless voice.

"Look, you know we don't have enough kids. What do you want me to do, forfeit the season?"

But the man persisted, "Well, I sure wouldn't be lookin' over there, that's for sure."

Around the room, there was a chorus of agreement as several of the men nodded. Every eye was on Bill. The room became dead silent.

Bill looked at their blank faces.

Outside, the whistle blew, signifying the end of the break. Bill seemed relieved to hear the sound of it.

Gradually, the men all got up and went back to work, but Bill lingered. And as the men left, a few privately patted him on the shoulder as if to offer support, including Dale. But this was of little consolation to Bill Campbell. For that day—when it really mattered—no one had spoken up. No one had come to his defense.

Bill watched as Joe walked back to his table, grabbed his things and left the room. As he passed by, Bill felt the weight of the world on his shoulders. He thought he was going to be sick. He felt horrible. *Could everyone be that prejudiced?* The thought weighed heavy on Bill's mind.

He hoped not.

That afternoon, Bill worked alone. He climbed several oil storage tanks, checked their gauges, and recorded his findings. By the end of the day, he was looking forward to going home.

Then there was practice—he still had to attend at four o'clock. *But what was the use,* he thought. On Thursday morning—in exactly two days—the final rosters had to be turned in. As things stood now, Bill was still three kids short.

Just before three o'clock, Bill finished logging his results and hung his clipboard on the wall. He picked up his lunch pail, walked over to the time-clock, and waited. Standing a few feet away were Dale and Roger. They had been talking, but seeing Bill, they abruptly ended their conversation.

As the whistle prepared to blow ending the shift, Bill looked at Dale and made brief eye contact with him. The tension between them seemed thicker than ever.

Bill looked at his watch as the second hand hit the 12. It was three o'clock. As if right on cue, the high-pitched steam whistle sounded out over the refinery.

Bill looked up at Dale, and broke the silence. "Right on time," Bill said. Dale looked at Bill. Bill looked him in the eye, "I better get goin'. See ya later."

Dale nodded. "Yeah, see ya later on."

Bill grabbed his time card, and punched the clock. He looked at Roger. "See ya Roj'."

Roger looked at him, and lowered his head. He kicked at a pebble with the toe of his boot. "Yeah, see you tomorrow."

Bill turned and walked away. Straight ahead was gate number Five.

As Dale watched Bill leave, he grabbed his time card, and waited his turn to clock out. As Bill got out of hearing range, he leaned toward Roger, and made his views plain.

"Like I told him, if he wants to stick his nose on that side of town, he can do it by himself. I don't want nothin' to do with it."

As Bill walked down the long narrow path leading out of the refinery that afternoon, he couldn't help but think of how he had been let down. He still considered Dale to be his best friend. In his heart, he knew Dale didn't hate black people, and he certainly wasn't a racist.

But Dale was like so many others—he was resistant to change. Just like so many others, he didn't like being pushed into it.

With the thought of losing his team in the back of his mind, Bill showed up at practice a little early. Dale showed up a little late. The two men had a long talk, aired out their differences, and things seemed to be back to normal between them.

That afternoon, after a good practice, a practice which Bill thought had been one of their best yet; Bill praised the boys for their hard work, and then dismissed them. After securing the practice equipment in the back of his truck, he headed for home. Kevin hopped on his bike, and did the same.

As Bill drove home, he went his usual route. And as he drove by the vacant lot adjacent to Market Street, he hoped to see the black boys. But as he arrived at the lot, he found it empty.

Bill sighed to himself, *They got to be somewhere,* he thought. Bill slowly circled the block a few times, but each time he saw nothing. He turned into a small corner store parking lot and backed up his truck in order to turn around.

Stretching his arm across the back of the seat, Bill looked into his rear view mirror. Something caught his eye. That something was Charles Taylor.

He was standing in the doorway, having just exited the store. He had a piece of gum in his hand. He was unwrapping it. Bill immediately hit the brake, and stopped the truck. As he observed Charles for a moment, Bill nervously tapped the steering wheel with his fingers. Charles began to walk.

Bill exhaled and shook his head. The scene in the break room earlier in the day was playing over and over again in his mind. The voices were angry. They tormented him. Bill suddenly felt indecisive; his mind was in a quandary. *Should he do it, or shouldn't he?* he wondered.

In a moment of angst, Bill decided to go for it. He put the truck in park, and slammed the emergency brake to the floor. He opened the door, stepped out of the truck, and made a beeline at Charles.

"Hey! You gotta minute?" Bill stepped closer. Charles froze in his tracks. "I saw you playin' ball the other day, you and some of your friends. What grade are you in anyway?"

Charles looked a little unsettled. He looked to the left and then to his right, and slowly responded, "Sixth."

Bill's eyes lit up. "Did you say *sixth*?"

Charles nodded.

"You ever thought about playin' football, organized football?" Bill asked.

Charles looked puzzled. "You mean for a team?"

Bill nodded. "Yeah, for a team."

Charles looked interested. "Are you a coach or somethin'?"

Bill nodded. "Yep."

Charles thought about it for a moment, and then frowned a little, "I—I don't think my daddy would let me."

Bill looked him in the eye. "Well maybe I could talk to your daddy. Where do you live anyway?"

As Bill and Charles arrived in the truck in front of Charles Taylor's house, Bill thought it might be a good idea if he waited outside. So Charles opened the door, got out of the truck, and walked to the front door alone.

Bill watched anxiously as he disappeared inside.

After a few moments, Charles reappeared with his father, a neatly- dressed black man about 35 years old. His sharp chiseled features reminded him of Charles. Bill could see the resemblance. They looked a lot alike. Bill quickly got out of the truck, and approached them.

If Bill felt a little awkward, it showed, as he struggled to get his first few words out of his mouth, "Hi," Bill stuttered. "I saw Charles, and a few other boys playin' ball the other day," Bill said. He then extended his hand, "I'm Bill Campbell, by the way."

Charles' father looked a little suspicious. He slowly extended his hand, and shook Bill's.

"Mr. Taylor, right?" Bill asked.

Mr. Taylor nodded.

"Pleased to meet ya. Like I said, I saw your boy playin' ball the other day and he looked to be the right age. I thought I might ask if he wanted to play."

Mr. Taylor looked surprised. "For you?" he asked.

Bill gently nodded. Mr. Taylor looked down at his son. Charles eyes lit up.

Mr. Taylor was unsure. "Well, I don't know about that," he said.

Bill looked at Charles, and pressed on. "Well, your boy does have some talent, and we sure could use him."

Charles gave his father an inquisitive look, but Mr. Taylor still wasn't sure. "Can you do that?" he asked.

Bill shrugged. "I don't see why not, you're in our district."

Mr. Taylor looked surprised, "We are?" Bill nodded.

Mr. Taylor looked down at his son. "I—I don't know."

Bill continued, "Look, I only got 15 kids. I could really use some help."

Charles looked up at his father once more. "Com'on daddy, can I? You know I can do it."

Mr. Taylor still looked unsure.

Bill backed off a little, "You think about it," Bill said. He then started to back away towards his truck. "We practice across from the baseball diamond next to Adam's Elementary. Four o'clock. You don't need to bring anything, we got all the equipment."

Mr. Taylor gently nodded, put his hand on Charles' shoulder, and turned him toward the house. As they walked away, Bill got in his truck, and turned the key in the ignition and put it in drive.

He planted the seed, he thought. Now all he needed was a harvest.

That night, Bill hardly slept. By the time he arrived at the practice field Wednesday afternoon, he was dog-tired. When

Dale showed up, Bill told him what he had done—how he had gone to Charles' house, but Dale remained skeptical. Nevertheless, Dale apologized further about what had happened, and he promised to be more supportive.

There was no sign of Charles, but Bill held out hope.

And what if he did show up, he thought, *they would still be two kids short.* Any way Bill sized it up, it was going to take a miracle to beat tomorrow's deadline.

As four o'clock came, Bill started the practice on time. Dale put the boys through their calisthenics. As the practice began in earnest, Bill had them line up on offense first.

Kevin lined up at quarterback, the only position he had ever played. Randy lined up at right tackle, something he wasn't too thrilled about. He wanted to play fullback, but with the shortage of kids, Bill had to put him on the line.

Laying on the ground, were a few foam rubber dummies that served as defenders. As Kevin took the first snap, he handed off to a running back who ran through the line in between two of the dummies.

Bill blew his whistle. "Okay, line it up, run it one more time," he instructed.

After a few more running plays, Bill decided to work on the passing game. He split Larry, their best receiver, out wide to the right.

With the snap of the ball, Kevin dropped back to pass. Larry ran downfield about fifteen yards, and then cut to the sideline.

"Square your shoulders!" Bill yelled out to Kevin.

Kevin heaved the ball toward Larry, but the pass wobbled badly and sailed well over his head.

Bill winced at the poor throw.

"Co'mon Kevin! Grip the ball!" Bill scolded.

The ball then rolled an additional 15 yards, and to Bill's pleasant surprise, it came to rest at the feet of one—Charles Taylor.

Charles and his father had quietly arrived at the practice. Charles bent over and picked up the ball. He tossed it to Larry, who then ran back to the huddle.

Bill smiled. Dale was genuinely surprised.

"Well, I'll be," Dale said.

Larry was surprised too, as he tossed the football to Bill.

"What's that colored boy doin' here?" Bill looked past Larry at Charles and his father.

"He's comin' out for our team," Bill replied. He then motioned for them to come on over.

As Dale took over the practice, Bill got down to business, and pulled out a box full of equipment from the back of his truck. He carefully sized Charles up, and gave him his equipment.

Charles put the pads in his pants, and slipped them on over his shorts. Bill laced up his shoulder pads, and then handed him his jersey.

He watched as Charles put in on.

Bill Campbell thought he had never seen a more refreshing sight as he looked at Charles, freshly decked out in a brand-new Oiler uniform. Bill personally selected number twenty-four;

it had been his old high school number. He hoped it would bring him luck.

On the field, nearby, the boys had just finished running a play. Across the way, a handful of white parents watched intently as Bill blew his whistle and walked with Charles toward the huddle.

"You ready?" Bill asked him. Charles nodded. "Why don't you start out at receiver for now." Bill added.

Charles put on his helmet, and trotted to the huddle.

CHAPTER SIX

If the sight of Charles Taylor had rejuvenated Bill's soul, what he saw next, sent chills down his spine. On the opposite side of the field, at the edge of it, a pickup truck had come hastily to a stop in a cloud of dust.

A man—rather agitated—got out. It was Joe Carter, the father of the Carter twins. Joe looked angry as he hurriedly walked across the field. Bill's heart sunk in his chest at the sight of him.

"Ohhh no," he sighed aloud. "Now what?"

A few moments later Joe arrived a few feet away from Bill. "What the hell are ya doin', Bill? Have you lost your cotton-pickin' mind? You can't let him play."

Bill nervously looked across the way at Charles' father. Mr Taylor was keeping his cool. Bill stepped toward Joe, and attempted to coax him away from the field.

"Why not Joe?"

Joe looked incredulous. "*Why not?* Open your eyes!"

Bill stepped closer. "Look Joe, we don't have enough for a team as it is. He's in our district, he's got a right to be here."

Joe glanced at Charles, and then looked Bill back in the eye, "He may got a right, but I'm not lettin' my boys play with 'em!"

Joe motioned at his two boys. "Com'on."

The two boys looked at Bill, they were a bit unsure.

Joe glared at them, and gnashed his teeth. "*Com'on,* damn it!"

The boys looked disappointed, but gave in, and followed their father as he began to leave.

Bill exhaled, and threw up his hands. "Com'on Joe, be reasonable." He started to follow after them. "Com'on Joe, its 1964 for Pete's sake!"

But as Joe left the field with his two boys in tow, he never looked back. Bill watched in disbelief. He couldn't believe it. In frustration he shoved his hand into the air at Joe, "Ahh, who needs ya anyway!"

Dale looked at Bill with a look that seemed to say, *We do.* Bill shook his head. He turned and looked at the half- dozen remaining white parents. A few were shaking their heads too. They were talking among themselves. Bill looked at Charles' father. His face was blank, expressionless.

On the field, the boys looked stunned. Bill was too.

"I just don't believe this," he muttered to himself.

Standing not far away, Dale shook his head and added it up. "Incredible," he said as he made eye contact with Bill. "Did I just miss something or do we only have 14 kids now?"

After a moment, Bill turned and walked back to his team. He looked them over. They were all dumbfounded.

Bill motioned to Charles. "You ready?"

Charles was motionless. He looked like he was in shock, so Bill walked over to him, and showed him where to line up. He then instructed him for a moment, and motioned at Kevin to run the play.

As the Oilers huddled up, the white players sized up Charles Taylor. Many, if not all, had never played with a black boy before.

As they broke the huddle, Bill backed out of the way. Charles split out wide to the right—just as Bill had showed him—and lined up at the line of scrimmage.

Kevin looked over at him and nodded. He then barked out his signals, and took the snap. As Charles ran the pass route, Kevin dropped back to pass, and threw the ball right to him.

Charles ran the route perfectly, but the ball hit him in the hands, and dropped to the turf.

Over and over, that afternoon, Charles Taylor ran different patterns, just as Bill had designed them. But each time, he dropped the ball. Finally, after about 10 attempts, Bill blew his whistle, and put him out of his misery.

Charles looked dejected, and the rest of the Oilers—they weren't too impressed.

Dale looked at Bill, and summed it up. "Look, I don't think this is gonna work. He'd have a better time catchin' a cold."

Bill began to look desperate. The white parents across the way were talking among themselves. They looked ripe for rebellion. There was mutiny in the air.

Bill knew he was in trouble. He looked at Charles' father. Mr. Taylor looked humiliated. Inside, Bill's stomach was in knots. His mind raced. In desperation, Bill looked over at Charles, and called out his name.

"Charles!"

Charles looked back, "Yes sir?"

Bill stepped toward him. "Think you can return a kick without getting tackled?" Charles shrugged.

Bill stepped closer. "Go on down the field a ways. I'm gonna kick it to ya."

Charles nodded and took off. Bill lined up the rest of the team in a straight line. They looked a little confused.

He then picked up the ball and faced them. "Now I'm gonna kick this ball to Charles—you all are gonna try to tackle him."

Many of the boys smiled, a few shook their heads. Randy nudged Kevin and smirked. "Ah man, this is gonna be a slaughter."

Dale thought he was crazy too. He looked at Bill like he'd lost his mind. "What are you doin now, tryin' to get the kid killed?"

Bill ignored him, but the rest of the boys seemed to agree. They rubbed their hands together, and licked their lips—as if they were preparing for a feast.

Bill had seen enough. He cupped his hands to his mouth, and called out to Charles. "Ready?"

Charles nodded. His eyes were as big as saucers. Bill took a step forward, and punted a high kick downfield. The remaining Oilers let out a loud yell, and began sprinting at him. About 40 yards downfield, the ball hit Charles squarely in the chest. He promptly dropped it, and then picked it up.

As the boys converged on him, Charles easily sidestepped the first few potential tacklers. He then promptly juked two more, leaving them grasping for air.

With a burst of speed, he sprinted to the sideline. The remaining tacklers converged like a swarm of mad bees. Suddenly, Charles stopped on a dime and cut against the grain. The defenders were caught off guard. Unable to stop their momentum, they began to plow into each other, and slide right by him.

Charles avoided the remnants of what was left, juked Randy, and sprinted toward Bill for an obvious touchdown. As he arrived across the line, Bill blew his whistle.

Dale's mouth was wide open. He looked over at Charles, and then back at Bill. "On the other hand," Dale said, "he might work out."

Bill looked relieved, and then genuinely happy. Dale was in awe. His mouth was agape. He just shook his head. Bill stepped toward Charles. "From now on son, you're a runnin' back!"

Charles smiled, and across the field his father did too. On the side of the field, the white parents were speechless.

Downfield, the rest of the "Oilers" made their way back to Bill, humbly. They were all looking at Charles, in awe of his revelation.

As the practice continued that day, Charles Taylor put on a show. And with each new run, Dale's countenance grew brighter. Even the white parents seemed to appreciate his talent.

When the practice finally concluded, and the boys were headed home, both Bill and Dale looked like new men. Off in the distance, Charles and his father exited the same way they had come. Dale stared after them for a moment, and then turned and faced Bill. "Man, we gotta get back over there, and get some more kids!"

Bill held back a smile, and dug at him. "I thought you said it wasn't a good idea."

But Dale was unmoved. "Are you kidding?' He pointed to the horizon at Charles and his dad. "That place is a gold mine! Why I've never seen nothin' like that before. Now *that's* talent!"

Again, Bill tried to conceal a smile, but he couldn't.

Twenty minutes later, Dale and Bill were back in the middle of "Colored Town." This time, Dale was leading the way. They drove in separate trucks. Dale pulled his truck next to the curb, and got out.

He could hardly control his excitement. Now he seemed oblivious to his environment. Bill parked behind him, and got out.

Dale was waiting, and he was hyped. "You take that side, I'll take this side," he said.

Bill smiled softly. He willingly agreed, and walked across the street. Dale made his way to the first available house, and knocked on the door. Bill did the same.

Initially, the going was tough, but Dale was persistent. He appeared rather animated as he spoke with a mother, and measured her two boys with his hand.

On the other side of the street, Bill talked to a father who was nodding. Throughout the neighborhood, kids were running everywhere.

In the back of Dale's truck one solitary boy sat, then another, and another. But Dale wasn't finished, and neither was Bill, as they continued knocking on doors, and talking to groups of kids.

Finally, after two hours canvassing the neighborhood, Dale had accomplished his goal. In the back of his truck, there wasn't room for one more. Bill had faired about as well.

The back of his truck was full too.

Leaving Colored Town that day, Bill's thoughts turned to the season, and Darrell Phipps. He wondered what Darrell would say if he could see him now? It must have looked like an odd sight. Two pick up trucks, with white men driving, crammed full of smiling black boys.

A few minutes later, Bill and Dale arrived at Bill's house, and quickly got to down to work. In the middle of Bill's front yard, he and Dale pulled equipment out of boxes, and sized up each boy.

Exiting the front screen door was Mary. There were black boys everywhere. She looked over at Bill. He was pulling out a pair of shoulder pads from a box. Bill looked up at her.

Mary's mouth was agape. "You did it," she said. "You actually did it."

Bill smiled. "Yep."

Mary stepped off the porch, and walked over to where Bill was standing. As she did, the swarm of boys seemed to part like the Red Sea, and made a way for her. As she approached Bill, she looked in amazement at the many faces. She then looked at Bill.

"Need some help?" she asked.

Bill shrugged. "Sure," he said.

All around the neighborhood people were coming out their front screen doors. Many were already standing in the street, and some were standing in their front yards.

All were either talking about, or gawking, at the sight. In the middle of the yard, Mary approached one of the boys. She had a black marking pen and a roll of white tape in her hand.

"What's your name?" she asked him.

The boy looked at her. "Thomas, Thomas Cahill," he said. Mary smiled and wrote his name across the white tape.

On the street next to the curb, Randy stood straddling his bike watching all of the activity. Next to him, Kevin was watching too. "I know they all got names, but I can't tell 'em apart," Kevin said.

Randy slowly shook his head, "Yeah, me either."

Friday morning, Bill woke up early and ate breakfast alone. He got in his truck, and headed off to work. As he arrived at the refinery, the sun was beginning to rise in the eastern sky. In the distance, the oil storage tanks reflected the golden hue of the early morning light.

Entering gate number Five, Bill flashed his nametag at the security guard, and made his way to the time clock.

He was fourth in line. Bill waited his turn to punch in. Up ahead, Ed the union rep, had his hands on his hips. He was waiting for Bill. He looked anxious. Something was obviously on his mind. His eyes kept moving from side to side.

Bill punched the clock and put his card back in the rack.

"Bill, you got a second?" Ed asked.

Bill looked him in the eye—something was definitely wrong. "Yeah. What's up?" Bill replied.

Ed motioned over his shoulder with his head. "I need to see ya in my office," he said sharply. Ed turned and began walking up the stairs. As Bill followed him up the stairs, he thought, *Oh great, now what?*

Standing inside the union office overlooking the refinery, Bill knew he was in trouble. He just didn't know what for. While Ed shut the door for privacy, Bill pulled out a chair in front of Ed's desk.

Ed looked edgy as he walked over and sat behind it. He looked straight at Bill. "You really know how to stir things up don't ya?" he blurted out.

"What are you talkin' about, Ed?"

"*You know* what I'm talkin' about," Ed said with emphasis.

Bill did know—and his pale face showed it.

Ed continued. "I must have got six phone calls last night from hard- workin' union members, tellin' me their dues money was bein' used to sponsor a colored team! Is that right?" Ed asked.

Bill did not respond. Ed stood up. He looked concerned.

"Now look Bill, I could personally care less who you put on your team, but you've gone and put my butt in a real bind here. And we're gonna have to do somethin' about it."

Bill leaned forward a little. "Well what am I supposed to do, Ed—you already gave me the money."

Ed sighed. "You could give it back?"

Bill looked incredulous.

"Or lose the colored boys." Ed countered.

Bill's face was turning red. He shook his head, and leaned back in his chair. "Huh uh, *no way*," Bill said emphatically. Bill shook his finger at Ed. "We made a deal —remember?"

Now Ed's face was turning red.

Bill continued. "And besides Ed, if you haven't forgot, it's my butt that's on the line here, too," Bill reminded him.

Ed leaned forward and put his hands on the edge of the desk. "Yeah Bill, it is, *it sure the hell is*," Ed said with anger.

With that, Bill's fate was sealed. Bill had committed the unpardonable sin. He had crossed Ed Rivers. And now he would pay the price.

For this, Bill was sentenced to three days in Refinery Hell. In the belly of the most God- forsaken place on the face of the Earth.

Within 30 minutes, the sentence would be carried out, as like a lamb led to the slaughter, Ed marched Bill to the tanks, and notified the shift boss of his decision.

"Three days," Ed told him. "We'll see how he likes it then."

A few minutes later, as Ed watched nearby, the shift boss pushed the handle of a scoop shovel at Bill.

"Go on, take it," the boss said. Bill looked him in the eye, and with contempt, he grudgingly accepted it.

As Bill stepped inside the open portal of the near empty oil storage tank, he was greeted by the smell of rotting crude.

And inside that tank, for the next three days, Bill would work alone. And work he did, scooping up thick and gooey remnants of crude oil with a scoop shovel. By the end of each day, his face and hands would be nearly blackened. It was stifling hot, grueling, and exhausting work.

On the third day, at the end of his shift—with his hands swollen and bleeding—Bill Campbell looked up at the heavens through an open portal of the now- empty tank.

As he heard the echoing sound of the shrieking steam whistle, and looked up through the porthole at the deep blue sky, his soul was cleansed. And as the sound of the whistle faded away, signifying the end of the shift, for Bill, it was as if God had raised him from the dead.

Sweating profusely, with his face and hands were nearly blackened, Bill stepped outside the tank, and shielded his eyes from the blinding sun. He was exhausted. He looked down at his bleeding hands. They were almost numb.

By Monday afternoon, at four o'clock, twenty-eight boys gathered on the grassy field of Adams Elementary. By the looks of them, they all seemed to be having fun. Some were playing catch with footballs, others were standing around talking. Still a few were wrestling around on the ground.

For the most part, the boys had already fully integrated themselves. Across each of the newest boys' helmets was a piece of white tape with their last name on it.

On one side of the field, there stood a group of black parents. On the other side were a group of white parents. Bill stepped forward, and blew his whistle to get their attention.

"Bring it in." The boys began to gather around. "Everyone, take a knee," Bill said.

The boys quickly complied, and took a knee in front of Bill and Dale. Bill looked proud.

"All right you guys, listen up. If you haven't already noticed, we got a whole bunch of new teammates."

The black boys were beaming from ear- to- ear. Dale was too. All eyes were fixed upon Bill.

"This is *our* team now." Bill spread his arms wide. "We are the Oilers!" Bill announced. "And we're gonna be good—that is if we learn to play together."

Bill walked over to Charles, and looked down at him.

"Now we got less than a week before our first game, and some of us have a lot of catchin' up to do." Bill looked back up at the rest of the team. "But right now I want all the new kids to stand up and introduce themselves."

Bill stepped back, and motioned to a rather large boy.

He looked around, and then slowly stood up. "I'm Samuel Ellis, and I'm pleased to meet ya."

He kneeled back down, as a boy beside him stood up.

"I'm Thomas Cahill." Thomas sat back down, while another boy rose to his feet.

"I'm Carl Stewart." Carl knelt back down, and one- by- one, each of the other boys stood up and announced their names. The pace seemed to quicken as each new boy stood to his feet.

Finally, Charles stood up, smiling so big his face was about to break. "I'm Charles Taylor."

Randy had heard enough, "Ahhh, sit down!"

All of the boys began breaking up in laughter. Charles needed no introduction!

CHAPTER SEVEN

With the start of the Pee Wee football season only a few days away, Bill Campbell and Dale Edwards had a lot to think about. Mainly, where would they put the new kids?

None of them knew any of the plays, except for Charles, and he knew very few. So after a good night's sleep, Bill and Dale put their heads together and decided they would integrate the new kids into the defense first, where, as Dale put it, "It was more self- explanatory."

Except for Samuel Ellis, who Dale said, "He's the biggest fifth grader I ever saw." And Bill agreed. They would put Samuel on the offensive line and tell him to—as Dale said, "Just knock 'em down son."

Traditionally, the start of the fifth- and sixth-grade football season began on the second Thursday of September. For the past 12 years, boys from 11 area grade schools had come together at PAL field in order to compete in the citywide league.

It was full- contact football.

For many, PAL field had come to be a symbol of unity in this small town. Here it didn't matter where you lived or what your family's income was. It was a place where poor kids and rich kids could come together, forget their community status for an hour, and just play football.

But in reality, the season took on a very different meaning. The East side took particular pride in the fact they usually had the better athletes. The season afforded them the opportunity to showcase their talents.

The West side looked forward to the competition too, and took pride in the fact they had the better schools. Now it seemed, with their enrollment booming, the West side schools were gaining the upper hand on the field too.

It was a fact that stuck in the craw of the likes of Dale and Bill.

PAL field itself, was only 80 yards long. It was shortened for the sake of competition. Overlooking the north end zone of the field was a huge gravel rock pile, compliments of a local quarry.

To the west was the city water works. Not far from there, were several sets of railroad tracks leading to two towering grain elevators. They were a prime source of community revenue.

And so as game day came, Bill and Dale were ready—or at least they hoped they were. Their rocky start had put them at a disadvantage—but they had worked hard, and for the moment, they felt prepared.

Arriving at PAL field at a quarter past five, Bill met Dale in the gravel parking lot adjacent to the field, and went over the evening schedule.

The Oilers were playing the early game, scheduled to start at six. The first order of business was to put the boys through their pre-game warm-ups. By 5:30, with most of the team having already arrived, Bill asked Dale to assemble the boys between the 20 and 40-yard line.

As they took the field for the very first time, Bill could not help but feel proud at the sight. The United Oil Workers Union Oilers looked like something out of the future—wearing their black game jerseys with gold numbers, white pants with a black stripe, and brand new black shiny helmets.

While Dale led the team through their drills, Bill stood off at a distance and observed. He was also looking at their opponent for the evening, the Coolidge Steelers, wearing white jersey's with black numbers, white pants, and white helmets with a black stripe down the middle. They were also preparing for the game.

Behind Bill, were the bleachers, able to accommodate about 150 people. They were about half full. But many people were still arriving.

On the upper left side of the bleachers, sat a handful of black parents. They were totally separated from the rest of the crowd. Seated among them was Charles Taylor's mother, Leona and her three little boys.

As Mary began to ascend the bleachers with little Rebecca at her side, she looked up at them and faintly smiled. About six rows up, sat an elderly white couple. The woman looked at the black parents. She seemed surprised to see them. She nudged her husband, a man about 65 with thinning gray hair and tanned leather skin.

"Henry, what are those colored people doin' here?" she asked.

Henry looked at them, as Mary looked for a place to sit down.

"Beats me," he said.

His wife looked back onto the field. "Why that team's got colored boys on it!"

Mary started to sit down, but she paused and looked at the woman. Henry raised a pair of binoculars to his eyes and then lowered them. "Well I'll be, they sure do." He shook his head. "What's this world comin' too anyway?"

Mary could not believe her ears. She looked at the man with disbelief and shook her head. "I think it's called progress!" she impulsively replied.

The man was a bit taken aback. Mary frowned a little at him and then looked at the black parents. They were stone faced. She then looked down at little Rebecca. "Com'on honey."

Mary grabbed her little hand, and began ascending the bleachers to where the black parents sat. As if on cue, as they walked up the steps, Rebecca turned her head, made an awful face, and stuck out her tongue at the elderly man. Mary caught her in the act.

"Stop that!" Mary scolded her.

Henry's eyes widened a little. He made a face right back at her. Mary rolled her eyes and threw up her hands.

"Oh grow up!" Mary added.

As Mary ascended the bleachers, she looked several white parents in the eye. A few were smiling. Passing by them, Mary made her way to Charles' mother.

She extended her hand. "Hi. I'm Mary Campbell. Bill's wife."

Leona smiled and extended her hand. "I'm Leona Taylor, Charles' mother, nice to meet ya," she said.

Mary smiled and replied. "Nice to meet you."

Mrs. Taylor made room for Mary and Rebecca, and they sat down.

Below the stands and to the right was a little concession stand that seemed to be doing a brisk business. Above the stands, was a small press box, wherein sat two gentlemen. One was the announcer; the other kept the clock and the scoreboard, which was situated behind the north end zone. Beside the stands were two tall light standards able to illuminate the entire field. As the clock ticked down to zero, and the horn sounded, the Oilers broke off from their drills and made their way to the sideline in front of the stands. It was game time.

As the two teams occupied their sidelines, a referee approached each team and escorted the team captains to the center of the field. The opponents then shook hands and took opposite sides of the shortened gridiron. An official then tossed a coin into the air. It landed on the turf. The Steelers won the toss. They elected to receive.

On the Oiler sideline, Bill rallied the team and gave them their final instructions. He then sent the kickoff team onto the field. The last Oiler out was Carl Stewart, who promptly lined up in his position right in front of the Steeler bench.

As the two teams lined up ready for the opening kickoff, the Head Official blew his whistle, raised his arm and then dropped it.

The season was officially underway.

The Oiler kicker ran at the ball and booted a line drive about thirty yards downfield. After a few bounces, the Steeler's return man scooped it up and began to run up the field.

Streaking down the sideline, like a missile in flight, Carl Stewart met him full speed at about the 20-yard line. The sound of the hit echoed across the field. The boy smacked the turf, hard. It was a very good hit. Bill shook his head and looked at Dale. "Wow!" Bill said.

Bill Campbell had had butterflies in his stomach all afternoon. But as the game got underway in earnest, and the Steeler's ran their first play, Bill began to settle in. This was what it was all about—the sound of helmets colliding, and pads popping—the smell of the sod turf. To Bill Campbell, it didn't get much better than this.

The quarterback for the Steelers was a tall lanky kid. He had a good arm—Bill had seen him before. But for the time being, the Steelers were playing it safe. As the quarterback took the snap, he handed the ball to a running back who ran around the right end. But he didn't get far, for up stepped Carl Stewart once again. The *pop* of the pads could be heard across the field. On the sideline, Bill jabbed at the air, "Atta boy Carl, that's the way to stick 'em!"

Bill could already tell that the new kids had added intensity to his defense. Especially Carl Stewart, there was something special about him. He was not a particularly big kid, but he had good instincts, and a nose for the football.

A few plays later, the Steelers were forced to punt. And as the Oilers' offense took the field, Bill decided to start off with a quarterback keeper. It was a safe play, and he wanted to get off on the right foot. It was a good call, Kevin picked up eight yards as he took the snap from center and sprinted around the right end.

But on the very next play, as Kevin took the snap, someone missed a block, and Bill watched as he got nailed for a three yard loss.

Kevin hit the ground hard. Bill winced, "Ouch!"

Dale leaned over to Bill, "We gotta work on that."

Bill agreed.

The next play was a pitch sweep, but it only yielded a couple of yards, and the Oilers were forced to punt. As Bill called for the punter, he paced the sideline. Behind him, sitting on the bench was Charles Taylor.

That evening, the Steelers were the first to break the ice. Even though their defensive intensity was up, the Oilers were missing tackles left and right. Nevertheless, Bill had never had such team speed before. "We're fast," he told Dale. "But we can't tackle worth a flip."

And his kids were fast—faster than their opponents. The problem was, they weren't disciplined. They weren't breaking down to make their tackles. And mis-direction plays were killing them. They kept over running the ball.

Eventually, Bill could only watch in dismay, as one of the Steelers' running backs broke a tackle and then another and sprinted down the field. On the opponents sideline, the Steeler players became excited at the sight of the seasons first touchdown. Bill shook his head. "Man, we got to work on our tackling," he said to himself.

With the scoreboard showing the Steelers ahead six to zero, the clock ticked down. And as the first half ended, and the horn sounded, the Steelers headed for the south side of the field. They gathered around their coach in the corner of the end zone.

The Oilers made their way to the opposite end zone. As they did, Bill and Dale walked and discussed the first half.

"What do ya think about puttin' Charles in as Runnin' back?" Dale asked.

"I would but he doesn't know the plays yet." Bill responded.

Dale shook his head, "Heck, just giv'em the ball and tell him to run with it!"

Bill nodded. "We'll see," he said.

As half time came to an end, Bill thought about what Dale had said. He had purposely decided before the game not to put Charles in at Tailback, because he had not yet learned the position. Charles knew very few of the plays. Bobby Morgan knew them all. He was their starter the previous year. Bill feared that if he put Charles in, and he started making mistakes, it might hurt his confidence.

In the final analysis, Bill wanted to wait for the right time to put him in. He knew he could have an immediate impact. But in the back of Bill's mind he just wanted to play it safe and at least wait until Charles knew more of the plays.

In the end zone, Bill finished instructing the boys and then dismissed them to their bench. Across the way, the Steelers were on there way back to their sideline. As the horn sounded, Bill looked at his clipboard. "Kickoff receiving team," he announced. Several boys looked at him. Bill motioned for them to take the field. As they did, Bill looked out and began to count his players.

On the sideline, Charles stood in his new clean uniform. Bill finished counting and then looked at him. "Charles!" The boy looked over at Bill with excitement in his face. Bill stepped over to him, "Get in there and return that kick." Charles nodded and put on his helmet and sprinted onto the field. Bill then looked at the goal line. "Bobby! Move up to the wedge line and block for Charles." Bobby Morgan nodded and promptly moved up leaving Charles all alone at about the ten-yard line.

The Steeler's kicker was ready for the kickoff. He waited for the official to signal and then ran at the ball and kicked it end over end. The ball sailed over the wedge-line and took a few bounces in front of Charles. Charles moved forward and scooped it up. He took off at a trot, right into the oncoming defenders. As the first defender arrived, Charles promptly juked him, and left him grasping for air. The defenders knees buckled as he slipped to the turf. Up ahead, Randy flatttened another with a crunching block. Kevin leveled one too. Charles then quickly darted between two more defenders and broke into the clear.

As he approached mid-field, the crowd in the stands began to rise to their feet. Downfield only the kicker stood between Charles and the goal line, and he looked a little scared. Charles' speed was blinding. The kicker would have to tackle him, because no one else was going to catch him from behind.

As Charles crossed midfield, he ran straight at the kicker and lowered his shoulder as if he were going to take him on. But then, at the last second, he shook his hips, and bolted to the sideline. The poor kicker had no chance. He never touched him. Charles then turned on the speed and in a matter of a few moments arrived untouched in the end zone.

Back on the Oiler sideline, his Oiler teammates were jumping up and down. And Bill, who had been running down the sideline with Charles, raised both hands high above his head. "Yeah! Touchdown!" Bill exclaimed. "Thatta boy Charles, now we're talkin'!"

On the opposite sideline, the Steeler players looked bewildered. Their coach was stunned. "That oughtta be illegal," he muttered to himself.

In the stands, the crowd was buzzing.

The next time the Oilers got the ball, Bill changed his mind and put Charles in as a Running Back. He told Kevin to keep it simple. And they did. And as the game wore on, Bill watched a young star in the making. Time and again, Charles ran with the ball and evaded tacklers. With each new run, he seemed to gain more confidence.

On one such occasion, he gained about twenty yards before he was knocked out of bounds just inches short of the goal line. The official blew his whistle and spotted the ball. "Man that was close!" Dale observed.

The very next play, Kevin handed him the ball again. Charles ran to his right where he was hit hard at about the two-yard line. Knocked off balance, he managed to regain his footing enough to dive over the line. An official raised his hands, and signaled the touchdown. Bill was very animated. "Thatta boy Charles! Now we're talkin'."

With the scoreboard showing the score 14 to 12 in favor of the Oilers, time on the clock ticked down. Kevin lined up under center and took the final snap and fell to a knee. The clock ticked down to zero and the horn sounded. The contest was over. The Oilers had won their first game. After a brief celebration, the Oilers assembled at midfield and shook hands with their opponents. They then went to an end zone to hear from Bill.

Gathered around their coach, the boys were fully integrated. Their parents, however, were not. As if by choice, the two groups of parents had remained apart. Bill stepped forward and addressed the boys; "You all did a great job tonight."

Dale agreed, "Great job guys!"

The black and white faces were beaming with pride.

"You beat a good team tonight. I'm very proud of you." Bill slapped his hands together and dismissed the team. "Have a good weekend and I'll see you on Monday."

The boys got up and began to disperse. As they did, they were all talking about their conquest.

Friday had been a great day at school for Kevin Campbell. He was the quarterback of the *best team* in the league, or so he thought. And he made sure to let everyone else know about it. By the end of the day, Randy was just sick of it. "Ahhh give it a rest Campbell!" Randy said.

And by the time Monday afternoon rolled around, he and his fellow Oilers were champing at the bit to get better. Bill and Dale were too.

That afternoon, Bill decided to put his team through numerous tackling drills. It was a weak spot in their first game. He must teach them some discipline. He knew they would have to tackle better, if they wanted to keep winning.

The object of the drill at hand was for the running back to try to make it past a defender who stood between two foam rubber dummies. The dummies were placed about five yards apart. In anticipation, the defender moved his feet. On Bill's whistle, Dale tossed the runner the ball. In most cases, the runners were tackled. A few got by after contact. Charles Taylor made it through untouched nearly every time. Bill looked at Dale and shook his head. "He's got more moves than Carter's got liver pills." Bill said.

By Thursday evening, Bill Campbell had his team prepared. They'd had a good week of practice, and Bill thought they were much improved. They had also gotten some of the new boys into the offense, and Bill was anxious to see how it worked.

Arriving at PAL field at a quarter to six, the stands were nearly half full. And by game time, there wasn't a seat to be found. The games were always scheduled one hour apart. And with eight teams in the fifth and sixth grade league, the last game was usually underway by 9 o'clock. Today, the Oilers had the early game.

That evening, on the left upper side of the stands, the parents of the black children sat by themselves. All except for Mary and Becky Edwards, who were sitting next to Charles' mother and father and their three little boys.

On the field, the game was already in progress. Tonight's opponents were the Chiefs, decked out in their red jerseys, and white pants. The Oilers were in an offensive huddle. The Chiefs were lined up on defense. The scoreboard showed the Oilers were ahead 16-0.

In the middle of the huddle, Kevin knelt down. His eyes beamed with confidence. "Forty-six toss on two. Ready, break!" The Oilers broke the huddle, clapping their hands in unison. They lined up over the ball. Kevin stepped under center, glanced back at Charles, and then looked back over the defense. "Down! Settt! Hut, hut!" Kevin barked.

As the center snapped the ball, Kevin swiveled and pitched it back to Charles. Moving to his right, but looking downfield, Charles accelerated, sprinting for the sideline. As he turned upfield, a defender dove for his feet. Charles hop-stepped over him.

Downfield three more defenders converged. As they arrived, Charles tucked the ball under his arm, put on the brakes, and came to a sudden stop. The converging defenders froze in their tracks. Caught off guard, and unable to stop their forward momentum, they each slipped to the ground. The three defenders legs had turned to jelly. With a sudden burst of speed, Charles sprinted around them down the sideline.

Only two safeties remained between him and the goal line. They had the angle, and cautiously closed in. Ten yards later, nowhere else to go, Charles spun like a top and sidestepped one of them. He then juked hard left and nearly alluded the other before losing his own footing.

The official blew his whistle and spotted the ball. Charles had gained 35 yards. On the Oilers sideline, Bill had twisted and contorted with his every move. He was hoping that he might score, but was nevertheless happy with the big gain. "Thatta boy Charles!" Bill said.

On the opposite sideline, Ted Cummings looked on in amazement. He was the opposing coach and a good friend of Bill's. Ted turned to one of his assistants. "How did he do *that*?" Ted asked. The assistant just shook his head.

At the end of the third quarter, the Oilers fans had plenty to cheer about. In the stands, they were clapping their hands. On the field, the Oilers were congratulating Charles. At a distance, the scoreboard was changing from sixteen to twenty-two. The Oilers now led twenty-two to zero.

With the clock winding down, and the game nearly over, the Oilers were on defense. The Chiefs ran their final play. The horn sounded, and the Oilers began to celebrate. While they did, Bill and Ted each ran out to the middle of the field and shook hands.

"Good game, Ted."

Ted looked whipped, "Yeah, for you. Where did you get that kid anyway?"

Bill looked at his boys and then back at Ted, "You mean Charles?"

Ted looked at Charles and identified him, "Number twenty-four."

Bill nodded. "That's Charles."

Ted looked envious, "He's incredible. Must be nice to have a secret weapon?"

Bill nodded. "Yeah, he's a real sleeper."

Ted nodded. He looked very serious. "Believe me, you're gonna need him," he said. "We played McKinley in our opener and they slaughtered us forty-four zip."

Bill didn't look surprised, "Yeah, they always have a great team."

Ted agreed, and then motioned at his own boys, "Well, I better go talk to the troops, I'll see ya later."

Bill patted him on the shoulder. "See ya, Ted."

And with that, the two coaches parted. And as they did, Bill looked back over his shoulder at the scoreboard one more time. It said, *Oilers twenty-two, Chiefs zero.*

CHAPTER EIGHT

With two games down, and five to go, Bill Campbell and Dale Edwards felt like they had made great progress. The following Monday, he and Dale put the boys through their toughest practice of the season. They had worked hard up to this point, and Bill wasn't about to soften up. Dale was resolute too, and jested with Bill reminding him of their *loan* from the union. Bill still maintained it was a *commitment*. Nevertheless, together, he and Dale worked hard to prepare the team for their next game.

As Thursday night rolled around, the Oilers were slated for the late game. Bill preferred the later starts, because he liked playing under the lights. And to him, it always seemed to add a little more excitement to the contest. As usual, the stands were full that evening. And tonight, there was a very special guest, in the person of one Darrell Phipps.

Seated in the stands in the far upper right hand corner, Darrell Phipps fiddled with a clipboard in his hand. He seemed to be impatient for the game to start. Next to Darrell was Frank Felcher, his good friend and the father of Lance, one of Darrell's star athletes.

His team, the Knights, had played the early game, and defeated the Steelers sixty to zero. It was total domination. The Knights had scored on every possession. Their opponents had never crossed midfield. In fact, the Steelers, who were not a bad team at all, had only managed two first downs. The Knights defense was simply suffocating. And as of yet, they had not given up a single point.

In fact, when it came to football, Darrell Phipps was known to be unmerciful. He frequently ran up the score on his opponents. And it was not uncommon for one of his teams to score fifty or sixty points in a game. And normally, Darrell could care less about his future opponents. The outcomes of their games were rarely in doubt. But tonight was different; there was no question why he had stuck around. He had heard a lot about Bill's new team. A team, which he had initially been told, was having a hard time finding enough players. And he had also heard about their star running back, and he was there to check him out.

Tonight, the Oilers faced the Garfield Jets. On one side of the field, the Jets were decked out in their green and white jerseys, and were busy doing their pre-game drills. On the opposite side, the Oilers were sitting Indian style between the twenty and forty yard lines. They were doing stretching exercises. Dale was leading them.

Kevin and Randy sat side-by- side.

Kevin looked confident, "We can beat these guys," Kevin said.

Randy, went right to the point, "We better. I got a dollar ridin' on the game."

Kevin looked interested, "Oh yeah? Who'd ya bet?"

Randy looked proud, "My dad."

After a moment, Randy leaned toward Charles who was sitting up one row and to his left.

"Hey Charles!" Randy yelled.

Charles looked back.

"I'll give you a *quarter* for every touchdown you score," Randy offered.

Charles looked Randy in the eye, "Serious?"

Randy looked at Kevin and then looked back at Charles and shrugged. "Sure." Randy said.

Charles thought about it for a moment. Randy smiled at Kevin. Dale spoke up, and got the boys attention, "All right everyone, on your feet."

As the game began, the Oilers won the toss and elected to receive the ball first. Bill started conservatively with a couple of running plays to the left side that yielded little gain. Dale couldn't understand the play selection and looked over at Bill and shrugged his shoulders as if to say, *what are you doing?* Bill looked back at Dale like *just relax will ya?* The two consecutive running plays to the left side, was setting up something, Dale could tell.

As Bill prepared to send in the next play, he grabbed a hold of Thomas Cahill's shoulder. The down marker showed third down and eight yards to go. On the field, the Oilers were gathering in their huddle. Kevin looked at his dad and waited.

Bill looked down at Thomas and gave him the play, "28 Reverse right on one." Thomas took a step onto the field then turned around realizing his number has been called.

There was excitement in his face, "28 Reverse Right?"

Bill nodded, "On one."

Thomas nodded and sprinted out to the huddle.

Breaking the huddle, the Oilers took to the line of scrimmage. Thomas lined up wide left as Kevin stepped under center. As the ball was snapped, Thomas began running at Kevin. Kevin faked the handoff to Charles over the left tackle. He then stepped out to hand Thomas the ball. But as he did, Thomas promptly ran right into him, and the ball squirted loose. A Jet defender quickly pounced on it.

As the official blew his whistle, the defender stood up and raised his trophy high in the air and celebrated. On the Oilers sideline Dale threw his clipboard down. Bill was wincing. Thomas had not gone wide enough and had blown the reverse. In the stands, Darrell Phipps and Frank Felcher were laughing hysterically.

On the field, Thomas made his way to the sideline, obviously feeling bad. Bill stepped out to meet him. "That's all right son, we'll get it right the next time." But Thomas was clearly disappointed. He walked to the bench and tossed his helmet down, and took a seat.

This would be the only miscue of the night for the United Oil Workers Union Oilers. And from then on, Bill knew right where to put the ball, squarely in the outstretched arms of one Charles Taylor. Shortly thereafter, he got his chance. Carl Stewart intercepted an errant pass and returned it to midfield.

On the sideline, Bill scrambled to send in a play. "Forty seven toss sweep on one," he said to Thomas. Thomas ran to the huddle and relayed the play to Kevin.

With the nose of the ball sitting on the Jets side of the forty-yard line, Kevin stepped under his center and barked out his signals. Taking the snap from the center, he quickly turned and pitched it to Charles who began running to his left. His strides were smooth and graceful. And as he approached the sideline, Bill instinctively took two steps back. From his vantage point, it seemed as if Charles was running right at him.

"Whoa," Bill said.

And as if on cue, Charles cut upfield, and then immediately cut against the grain. "Wow!" Bill added.

Like so many other times before, Charles quickness and agility had caught the defenders off guard. To a man, the Jets were left grasping for air. Charles turned on the speed and sprinted across the field to the goal line. And in a matter of a few seconds, he arrived in the end zone untouched. In the stands, Darrell Phipps looked impressed. He raised his eyebrows a little, and gave Frank a long look. Frank looked impressed too. He shook his head and jotted something down on the clipboard. There was no doubt about it, Charles Taylor was a force to be reckoned with. The scoreboard showed the Oilers at six, and the Jets zero.

As the first quarter drew to a close, the Oilers had the ball again. They were on the Jets one-yard line. And although everyone knew who was going to get the ball, it was an easy score. Kevin simply took the snap, faked to his left, and handed the ball back to Charles. He then watched as like a deer jumping a fence, Charles lept over the right side of the line. In the stands, Darrell watched too as the official raised his hands, and signaled the score.

A few minutes later, the Jets fumbled and the Oilers got the ball right back. Seizing the momentum, Bill quickly sent in the play, and called on Charles. Time and again, Kevin handed him the ball. Eventhough the Jets coach assigned two or three players to go where ever he went—it didn't matter. If he ran to the left, and found no hole, he would circle back to the right. Every time they seemed to have him hemmed in, he slipped away. And so it went, much to the chagrin of Darrell Phipps, who watched in amazement with everyone else as Charles sprinted down the sideline for a thirty-yard touchdown. The scoreboard now read twenty to nothing in favor of the Oilers. Darrell glanced at it.

He was looking a little worried.

In the second half, it was more of the same. Dale convinced Bill to let Charles have a try at returning a punt. Bill said he didn't want wear him out, but finally gave in. He then watched with a dropped jaw as Charles received a punt, and dazzled the crowd by returning it sixty yards for a touchdown. In the stands, Darrell stood looking on in disbelief. He glanced at Frank. Frank looked shell-shocked. The scoreboard now read twenty-eight to zero, Oilers.

After many congratulations, Charles Taylor made his way back to the sideline. Everyone was excited, except for Randy. He wasn't very happy. He now owed Charles four quarters, and the game wasn't over. Running side-by-side, as Charles ran off the field, Randy vented his concern, "Hey man, take it easy!" The expression on his face was priceless.

In the fourth quarter, Bill began to substitute many players freely. Although he didn't have many reserves, there were a few kids that had not had much playing time. With the ball on the Jets five-yard line, a few new players came out on the field and took their positions. The Oilers huddled around Kevin. He looked up at the new faces and smiled. Thomas brought in the play.

"Forty-eight toss on first sound," Thomas told Kevin.

Charles' eyes immediately lit up.

Randy grimaced, and began to whine. "Ahh man, not him again."

Kevin took charge. "Shut up will ya. Forty-eight toss on first sound. Ready break!"

The Oilers broke the huddle in unison. As they moved to the line of scrimmage, Kevin stepped under his center, and barked out his only signal. "Down!" The ball was snapped. Kevin quickly pitched it to Charles who ran to the right. Hit at the two-yard line, Charles bounced off the defender and sprinted for the corner flag and easily crossed the goal line. The official raised his hands signifying a touchdown. The scoreboard now read Oilers thirty-four Jets zero.

With the game winding down, and his attitude getting worse, Randy found himself sitting alone on the bench. He was not a happy camper. And by the sounds of the cheers of his teammates and the crowd, something told him what had just happened.

Standing up, Randy craned his neck and looked out onto the field. For a moment, he looked like he was going to be sick. "Ah man, don't tell me he scored again," Randy whined. The scoreboard now read forty to nothing.

The announcer announced the obvious, "Scoring for the Oilers, number twenty-four, Charles Taylor." In the stands, Darrell Phipps was white as a sheet. He motioned to Frank, he had seen enough.

With the game over, Bill Campbell was beginning to believe that his new team could compete with McKinley elementary. Things seemed to be coming together quite nicely. They had improved every week. So as the team assembled in the south end zone, and knelt down on one knee, he told them so.

"Wow! What a game. You guys have improved 100 percent. And Charles what got into you?" Charles shrugged his shoulders. Some of the boys snickered, they all knew.

Bill continued, "Six touchdowns in one game, that's got to be a record." Randy scowled and looked away. Bill finished up, "There's no practice tomorrow, so enjoy your weekend and I'll see ya on Monday."

Dale added, "Great game guys."

And with that they released the team. As the boys got up to leave, Kevin walked over to Charles, and extended his hand. "Good game, man."

Larry did the same. "Yeah, good game."

Charles smiled and nodded.

CHAPTER NINE

With three games under their belt, Bill and Dale's confidence was soaring. At the refinery, the word had gotten around that the Oilers were a pretty good team.

Even Roger was impressed. And Bill no longer dodged eye contact with his fellow co-workers. If anything, those who had opposed him were ashamed of their actions. Even Dale was a bit more repentant about his early opposition.

For Bill, none of this mattered. All he wanted now was the championship, and to beat Darrell Phipps.

With the more difficult part of their schedule coming up, and three more games remaining before their showdown with the Knights, Bill was not about to rest upon his laurels. If there was one deficiency, he thought, it was the offense.

They had become a one-dimensional team, relying too much on the athleticism of Charles Taylor. Bill knew he had to *open up* the offense, and thus he determined to put in a few new plays.

Before practice began, Charles reminded Randy of some unfinished business. With Thomas and Carl acting as a shield, Randy reluctantly placed six quarters one-by-one into the outstretched palm of Charles' hand.

Behind them, the rest of the team was lining up for calisthenics. Bill impatiently looked over at the four boys. He was completely unaware of what was transacting.

With the six new, shiny quarters tucked safely away in the bottom of his shoe, Charles joined his teammates on the practice field. For Charles it was no small amount of money. The feel of the quarters on the sole of his foot made him smile as he entered the offensive huddle.

That afternoon, Bill and Dale concentrated on the passing game. Kevin must have thrown at least 70 passes. After a dozen wind sprints, Kevin's rear end was dragging. Bill ended the practice and dismissed the boys. They began to disperse.

"Charles," Bill got his attention. "Give Kevin a hand, will ya?"

The field was littered with equipment.

Charles nodded, "Sure."

He and Kevin gathered up the orange cones, and practice dummies tossing them into the back of Bill's truck. As they finished, Charles said goodbye. "See ya tomorrow."

Kevin nodded, appreciating the help, "Yeah, see ya."

Bill said goodbye too. "See ya, Charles."

Bill and Kevin got into the pickup and began to leave. Charles picked up his helmet and shoulder pads draped with his jersey. He pulled the facemask of the helmet through the neck of the jersey. Grabbing the mask like the handle of a suitcase—he began to walk home across the vacant field.

After walking about four blocks, Charles stopped momentarily. He pulled off his shoe, and collected the six quarters placed under the sole. He put his shoe back on, and began walking again.

Up ahead, about three blocks, he could see Market Street. On the other side was his home. He looked down at the six silver quarters in his hand. They were shining. He admired them. He began walking again.

As he walked, from behind him, a red, late- model pickup appeared less than a block away. The truck slowly advanced.

At first, Charles seemed unaware it. But after awhile, he began to feel like he was being followed.

He was.

With an uncomfortable feeling gnawing at him, Charles glanced over his shoulder. He could see the truck slowly advancing.

As if the driver knew he had been spotted, he pulled the truck over next to the curb. Charles looked ahead; Market Street was only two blocks away. He began to quicken his pace. The truck began to move again.

Charles seemed to know it. He was starting to feel afraid.

Without warning, just as he had appeared, the red pickup disappeared. Charles glanced back. It was gone. He began to relax a little. *It might have just been coincidental,* he thought. Up ahead, Market Street was only a block and a half away. He stacked the six quarters in the palm of his hand and clutched them tightly. He was beginning to feel a little safer.

Suddenly, up ahead, the red pickup reappeared from a side street.

At the sight of it, Charles froze in his tracks. The truck wasn't moving. It seemed as if the driver was staring right at him. Its front-chromed grill shined in the afternoon sun.

The truck slowly turned onto the street.

To Charles it seemed as if the truck was coming right at him, but he wasn't sure. He began to panic. His instincts took over. Without even thinking, he turned into an alleyway and began to run. His equipment banged against his side of his thigh.

As he ran, he periodically looked back over his shoulder, but the truck wasn't following. About half way down the alley he slowed down to a jog, and then to a walk. His ribs ached.

Dogs from various back yards were now barking. Charles shook his head. He longed for home. Beads of sweat accumulated on his worried brow.

As he approached the end of the alley, Charles looked back over his shoulder one last time, but he saw nothing. Then, as he turned back around, he was confronted with the *object of his fear*.

The red pickup truck had reappeared. It was sitting in the mouth of the alley, its shiny chrome grill gleaming in the sun.

Charles swallowed hard as it inched a little closer to him. It seemed as if he were staring into the mouth of a caged animal. The engine roared like a lion.

His exit was blocked.

Terrified, Charles turned, and began running back the same way he came. This time, the truck followed him. It was accelerating. Charles sprinted as fast as he could down the alley.

Inside his chest, his heart pounded. Behind him, the engine of the truck revved as it changed gears. Charles looked back. It was gaining on him. With a burst of acceleration the truck halved the distance between them. Less than 50 feet now separated them.

Half way down the alley, Charles glanced back one more time at the gaining truck. It shifted gears. Charles eyes were wide with fear. Charles reached for another gear too, but suddenly, his feet tangled—and he tripped.

Having lost his balance, Charles braced for the fall. His equipment went sprawling, and as he hit the ground, the six quarters in the palm of his hand flew out, and landed in the dust.

The truck was all over him.

Like a lightening bolt, Charles gathered his feet, and bolted from the ground, leaving his money and equipment behind. He then sprinted faster than he ever had before. As he reached the end of the alley, he glanced to his left, and dashed out into the street. To his right was an oncoming car. The sound of screeching tires filled his ears.

He was about to be hit.

With the car horn blaring in his ears, Charles swallowed his fear and darted across the road. Once onto the sidewalk, he ran toward Market Street as fast as he could. He didn't stop running until he had reached the other side.

Back at the entrance to the alley, the red pick-up sat and watched Charles Taylor run. After awhile, it pulled out into the street. In the bed of the truck was Charles' equipment, still draped with his jersey number twenty-four.

The following day, practice began at the usual time. It was four o'clock. Dale led the boys through their drills. Bill stood alone scanning the horizon. He looked pensive.

Charles was nowhere to be seen.

By 4:30, Bill became even more concerned. Something was wrong, he could feel it. After awhile he called the team over, and began to question Thomas and Carl.

"Was he at school today?"

The boys looked at each other. Thomas responded, "Yeah."

Carl nodded. Samuel did too.

"Well, did he get sick or somethin'?"

Carl shook his head, "No."

Thomas agreed, "I don't think so."

Bill remained puzzled. "Huh, oh well, maybe he's just runnin' a little late."

Bill looked at his watch. It was nearly 4:45. He looked at the rest of the boys. "All right, offense with me, defense with Coach Edwards."

Bill slapped his hands together, and the boys broke off into two groups.

As the practice concluded, there was still no sign of Charles. Bill was mystified. Dale was concerned too.

Bill faced Dale. "I think I'm going to go check on him."

"That's probably a pretty good idea," Dale said.

Bill nodded, and patted Dale on the shoulder. "See ya tomorrow."

Dale said, "Yeah, see ya."

That afternoon, Bill got in his truck and proceeded directly to Charles' house. Arriving there, he got out, shut the door to his truck, and walked to the front porch. He knocked on the door and looked around.

After a few moments, Charles' mother came to the door.

"Hi," Bill said. "How ya doin'?"

"Fine," she said. Mrs. Taylor looked surprised to see him. It showed in her voice.

Bill continued. "I was lookin' for Charles, is he around?"

Mrs. Taylor gently shook her head "No, no he's not here. I thought he was at practice."

Bill seemed very concerned. "Huh uh, he didn't show up today, and nobody seemed to know where he was."

Mrs. Taylor seemed to be more puzzled than anything. "Well that's strange, he came right home after school and then left. I thought he was headed for practice."

Bill shook his head. "No. He didn't make it."

Mrs. Taylor looked out over the neighborhood. "Huh, well I'm sure he'll be home in a little while, it's almost time for supper—and that child does not like to miss a meal."

Bill nodded. "Do you have any idea where he might have went?"

Mrs. Taylor thought for a moment. "Huh uh, you might try by the school, though."

Bill thanked her, and began to back away.

As Bill started to leave, Mrs. Taylor called out after him. "Listen, if you do see him, tell him supper's ready, will ya?"

Bill looked back, raised his hand and acknowledged her.

"Sure will," he said.

Arriving in front of Carver Elementary, Bill got out of his truck, and walked to the school. A few small children were playing on the sidewalk. Bill walked around them and headed toward the playground in the back. As he approached the back of the run down school building, Bill let out a sigh of relief.

There was Charles.

He was sitting on a cement slab with his back against the wall. He was tossing small pebbles at an imaginary target. Charles was wearing a white cut off T-shirt, and had on his grass- stained football pants.

Bill approached him. "Charles!"

Charles looked up, startled.

"What are you doin'? Where were you today anyway, we missed ya."

Charles stood up, wiping dust off himself. He stammered a little. "'I—I—I couldn't make it."

Bill looked incredulous. "You couldn't make it?"

Charles shook his head and looked down as if he were ashamed.

Bill pressed on. "Why?"

Charles remained evasive, "I just couldn't."

Bill shook his head. "There's got to be some reason."

Charles looked at Bill and then looked away. Bill stepped closer, "What's wrong, son?"

Charles finally gave in. "I lost my equipment."

Bill looked him over. "You lost your equipment? How did you do that?"

Charles lowered his head. His voice was stressed. "I just lost it," he said.

Charles looked down at his feet. He was in agony. Bill reached out and put his hand on his shoulder. "What's wrong, son?"

Charles had tears in his eyes. Bill tried to reassure him. "You can tell me."

After a moment, Charles looked up at Bill, and then explained. "Yesterday, I was comin' home from practice, and this red pickup started following me. I got real scared. He just wouldn't go away. He made me drop my equipment."

Bill shook his head. "Is that why you didn't come to practice today?"

Charles nodded. "I went back to look for it, but it was gone. I'll pay you back—I promise."

Bill shook his head. "That's not necessary, Charles. Did you see who it was?"

Charles shook his head, "Huh uh. It was a red pickup, honest!"

Bill exhaled. "I believe ya. Look, we got all the equipment we need. If somethin' like that happens, all you need to do is come tell me. I'm not gonna get mad at ya."

Bill looked at Charles like he would his own son. "Com'on, your mother's lookin' for ya. She said it was supper time."

Charles nodded and smiled, a little.

Bill had never dreamed someone would attempt to intimidate one of his players. As Charles more fully described to him what had happened, Bill burned with anger at the persons responsible. In fact, his anger and sense of helplessness tormented him all evening.

As the Campbell's sat down for supper that evening, Kevin knew something was wrong. His father never said a word. Mary was silent too. The only sound that could be heard at the table was that of silverware impacting ceramic plates.

As Kevin watched his father eating, he knew something bad had happened. He just didn't know what.

No one was talking.

Next to Kevin, Rebecca pressed her bowl against her lips and slurped the remnants of her soup. Kevin paused, and dug at his plate. He looked at his father. His face is ashen. Kevin had never seen him quite like that before. His hand was almost trembling.

That night as Bill went to bed, he thought to himself, *Someone had threatened one of his boys. The stakes had been raised. Somehow, some way, he would ante up.*

The following morning, Bill discussed what had happened with Roger and Dale during their morning break. Dale was incensed. He immediately accused Darrell. But Bill was more careful, and refused to speculate.

Roger asked him point blank. "So, who do you think it was?"

Bill took a sip of his coffee. "I don't know—but I'm gonna find out."

Dale looked interested. "How ya gonna do that?"

Bill looked straight ahead. "You'll see."

That afternoon, as practice concluded, Bill lingered on the practice field, and waited patiently for the boys to leave. He and Dale spoke for a few moments, and Dale got in his truck and left.

Bill asked Kevin to pick up the dummies, and put them in the back of the truck. Not far away, Charles and his mates, Thomas, Carl and Samuel prepared to leave.

Bill watched as Charles pulled off his new jersey and shoulder pads in one piece. Pulling the facemask of his helmet through the neck, he gripped it firmly. Bill had given him jersey number seven for the time being, but had promised to get him his old number back before Thursday night's game. In fact, Mary was already working on it. This was something that seemed to please Charles very much.

With his new equipment secured, Charles glanced at Bill, and then began to walk off the field with his schoolmates.

Bill bit at his lower lip, and then bellowed out his name. "Charles!"

Charles and the boys stopped, and turned around.

"Help Kevin out, will ya?"

Charles nodded and walked back to Kevin and set his equipment down. Bill looked at the remaining boys on the edge of the field.

"You all can go on."

The boys looked a little puzzled. Bill looked at Charles and nodded, slightly.

Charles looked at his friends. "Go on, I'll catch up with ya."

Thomas shook his head, shrugged his shoulders, and motioned at Carl and Samuel. They began to leave.

As Charles and Kevin threw the last of dummies into the back of Bill's truck, Bill surveyed the horizon of the practice field. It was empty now. With hands on hips, he looked at Charles.

"Hop on in and I'll give you a ride."

Charles nodded. Kevin smiled broadly, as he looked at his father with surprise.

Up to this day, Kevin had never ever ventured beyond Market Street into Colored Town. It just wasn't done. Upon hearing his father was about to give Charles a ride home, Kevin became excited. He couldn't have been happier.

He wanted to see where Charles lived. He always wanted to go to that side of town. After all, he had never quite figured out why he wasn't allowed to go over there in the first place. So as Kevin and Charles tossed their pads into the back of the truck and got in, Kevin was eager to get going.

It showed in his voice. "Lets hit the road!" he said.

After driving several blocks, Bill did the unexpected, and pulled the truck next to the curb. He asked Charles to get out.

Kevin was clearly disappointed. He looked at Bill with his mouth wide open in disbelief. Bill avoided eye contact, and looked straight at Charles.

Charles seemed to think nothing of it. However, he did seem a bit apprehensive as he grabbed his equipment from the back of the truck, and stepped back onto the sidewalk.

From across the cab, Bill leaned over, and looked him squarely in the eye. His voice was re-assuring. "See ya tomorrow, son."

Charles nodded, and swallowed hard. "Yeah."

As Bill pulled away from the curb, and drove away, Kevin looked out the side window at Charles. Charles lifted his hand as if to wave. *He looked a little afraid*, Kevin thought. Kevin still could not believe they had stopped and let him out.

As Bill and Kevin drove off, Charles watched from the sidewalk. One block later, the truck made a left turn and disappeared. Charles had been left alone to walk the remaining few blocks to Market Street.

Like the day before, the neighborhood appeared to be calm and quiet. Charles began to walk. He took a quick glance around, and then fixed his eyes on Market Street.

Suddenly, behind him—as if on a cue—the late model red Chevy pickup appeared from the mouth of an alley about a block behind.

Slowly turning onto the street, the truck began to follow Charles. It stalked him for a half of a block. With a burst of acceleration, the truck pulled up beside him.

From the dark crevices of the shadow- filled cab, a low scratchy voice drifted out. "Hey *boy*, you lost or somethin'?"

It was Frank Felcher. Charles froze in his tracks, and swallowed hard. He never saw him coming. Charles was petrified.

The neighborhood seemed even emptier, now—even the birds had stopped chirping. Charles looked around, but he was still alone. Fear became his companion, as Frank's cold, dark eyes seemed to grip his soul.

Suddenly, down the street, another truck appeared. It was about two blocks away and accelerating rapidly.

The truck was familiar and it gave Charles some relief. It was Bill and Kevin—and not far behind them was another truck. It was Dale's.

As Charles looked back, Frank glanced into his rear view mirror. He could see the approaching trucks, and he knew he was in trouble.

Glaring at Charles, he slammed into drive. With rubber burning, and a high-pitched squeal, he took off. The chase was on.

Kevin had never experienced anything like it. The look on his fathers face was something he had never seen before. He looked angry and determined.

Kevin braced himself against the dashboard of the pickup, as Bill leaned forward. He had the gas pedal slammed to the floor. Kevin held on for his life as the engine screamed for another gear.

Up ahead in the red pickup, Frank was moving very fast, shifting gears every few seconds. His tires screeched as he made a hard right turn. Behind him, Bill turned right with him.

"I gotcha now, you son of a bitch!" Bill blurted out.

Frank was petrified. In his rear view mirror, he could see Bill gaining on him. He was less than a half a block away. In desperation, Frank slammed on his brakes and made a sudden left turn onto an empty street.

The abrupt turn caught Bill off guard. He slammed on his brakes. The sudden deceleration slammed Kevin's forearms into the dashboard. Kevin recoiled back into his seat. Bill had overrun the turn. The screeching sound of the tires, and the acrid smell of burning rubber filled the air.

Up ahead Frank could see Market Street, and his escape. The light was still green.

Behind him, Bill hurriedly backed his truck up, and with the grind of the gears, and a burst of acceleration—he got back into the chase. He was only a block behind.

Up ahead, Frank hit the intersection of Market Street at a high rate of speed. The rear of his truck fishtailed as he made the turn around the corner.

Behind him, Bill had gained ground once more, but the traffic light ahead was turning yellow. Bill punched the accelerator to make it through—but it was too late, the light turned red before he could get to the corner.

Scott Staerkel

Bill slammed on the brakes and gripped the steering wheel hard. His truck slid into the intersection. Down Market Street, the red truck was getting away. Its taillights were glowing in the distance. Bill watched helplessly. The oncoming traffic had hemmed him in.

To avoid a collision with the oncoming cars, Bill quickly backed up. Several blocks down Market Street the red truck made a sudden right.

Bill pounded the steering wheel, and craned his head after the truck fading out of sight. Kevin looked stunned.

Bill looked at him, "You all right?"

Kevin's face was white as a sheet. He slowly nodded, but said nothing. He couldn't get his lips move. Inside his chest his heart was pounding.

Kevin had never been so scared—nor felt so alive in all his life.

Later that evening, Bill leaned against his truck parked next to the curb, talking with Dale. Kevin overheard them.

"Did you see who it was?" Dale asked.

"No. I didn't get a good enough look at him. But I don't think he'll be back. Whoever he was, he didn't want to talk about it."

After a moment, Dale realized he had forgotten about Charles. "Where's Charles?" he asked.

Bill reassured him, "I checked on him. He's okay"

Dale looked relieved. "Good, think he'll be all right?"

Bill nodded and poked at Dale. "What happened to you anyway?"

Dale shook his head. "Man, you were goin' too fast for me. My insurance ain't that good!"

CHAPTER TEN

It was late September. The leaves on the tall oak and elm trees surrounding the practice field adjacent to Adam's Elementary were beginning to change colors. The bright yellow, orange, and red hues were a sign to all fall had arrived.

There was a chill in the air as Bill and his Oilers prepared for their next game. With the incident of the red pickup fresh in his mind, Bill did his best to put the matter behind him.

The following day was game day, and the Oilers were slated to play another west- side team, the Cowboys.

The Cowboys were always good. Last year, Bill's third- and fourth- grade team had lost to them by 20 points; 34-14. It was one of their only two defeats. But this year, the Cowboys were a young team consisting mainly of fifth graders.

By contrast, Bill's team was older. With the addition of the new kids, all told, there were 19 sixth- graders and nine fifth-graders, including Kevin, Randy, and Paul.

As the game began, the Cowboys, dressed in silver and white uniforms, struck first. Driving the length of the field, they took an early six to zero lead.

The Oilers answered right back, as Kevin scored his first rushing touchdown of the year, breaking away for a 30-yard score. By half time, the Oilers had retaken the lead, and led 14 to six.

In the second half, Charles began to strut his stuff. He scored on two long runs. Kevin added another by tossing a touchdown pass. As the game ended, the Oilers had notched their fourth win. The final score was Oilers 34, Cowboys 12.

The following day after work, as was his routine, Bill got in his truck and headed straight for home. Arriving there, he parked in the driveway, got out, and walked to the front door.

Beside the door, perched just below eye level, Bill reached over and grabbed a handful of mail from the box. Opening the front door, Bill walked to the kitchen, and sat his lunch pail down on the kitchen table.

As he looked through a stack of mail, behind him, he could hear the front screen door as it opened. Kevin was home from school.

Bill came to a white envelope with no return address, he looked at it curiously. As he opened it, Kevin entered the kitchen and sat his "Superman" lunch box onto the table beside Bill's.

Kevin took off his jacket, and hung it on the chair next to his fathers. The boy watched as Bill looked shocked, and then angry, as he read the contents of the letter. Finishing it, Bill quickly stuffed the letter back into the envelope, and put it into his shirt pocket.

Kevin looked concerned. "What is it?" he asked.

Bill shook his head. "Nothin'. It's none of your concern."

But Kevin *was* concerned. He could tell by the look on his father's face that what ever was in the letter—it was not good.

That night at about 10 o'clock, the mystery was solved. In the living room, out of sight, Kevin listened as Bill and Mary sat at the kitchen table, and discussed the contents of the letter.

Mary held the letter in her hand. "Now who would write somethin' like this?" she asked. "Do you think it's the same guy?"

Bill looked puzzled. "I don't know, but I'd like to find out. What's wrong with people anyway?" Kevin wondered the same thing. And it only got worse.

On Monday, Bill came home to find his Mary almost in tears. They had received another letter. It was addressed to "Billy Boy" Campbell. There was no return address. Mary had known what it was the moment she saw it, and she had opened it. It was neatly typed, as had been the first letter, and it basically said the same thing:

"To the Nigger lover on Locust street: You may think your something hot, but the fact is you're really not. YOU'RE JUST POOR WHITE TRASH, and a nigger loving son of a bitch to boot. Do yourself a favor, Billy Boy, lose the niggers, or you'll wish you had."

Bill trembled with anger as he read the letter, and then put it away. Mary was worried sick. Bill tried to console her. That evening, as Bill and Mary discussed what—if anything—could be done about the hate mail, Kevin entered the room. Mary's demeanor immediately changed, and so did Bill's. But Kevin knew, and the letters kept coming -one about twice a week.

That same week, Bill tried to remain focused, but it was hard. The letters were getting on his nerves. On Thursday night, the Oilers played the Giants. It was a close contest; only for the fact Bill made several bad play calls. The game finally came down to a defensive stand.

With the Oilers leading just 16 to 12 late in the fourth quarter, the Giants were driving the ball inside the Oilers 10-yard line. On the second down, they had attempted a pass, and had almost scored, but the pass fell incomplete.

On the fourth down, with the ball on the six- yard line, fearing another pass, Bill took Carl out and put in an extra defensive back.

At the last moment, he changed his mind, sent Carl back in, and called for a blitz. The extra defensive back barely made it back off the field in time.

It was the right call though, as Carl blitzed from his linebacker position untouched, and smothered the quarterback draw. The Oilers held on and won the game, 16 to 12.

The following day, Friday, Bill and Dale sat alone at a table in the break room drinking coffee. They discussed the previous night's game. But Bill was preoccupied, and it showed in his face.

Dale sensed it. "Still gettin' them letters, huh?"

Bill nodded, and took a sip of coffee. "Yep." Bill stared off into the distance. "And I still have no idea who's doing it."

Dale leaned forward, and lowered his voice, "Maybe it's Joe?"

Bill looked up and glanced across the room at Joe who was also taking his break. "Maybe, maybe not," Bill mused.

Dale continued. "Well have you talked to the police yet?"

Bill nodded. "They can't do anything; it's not against the law to hate."

The following week, the hate mail continued. It was really starting to put a damper on Bill's spirit, although he tried not to show it. He just couldn't believe someone he knew, or someone who knew him, could stoop so low as to send him such filth.

And the threats were only getting worse.

On Monday afternoon, the Oilers began to prepare for the Vikings. It would be their last game before taking on the Knights.

Bill reminded his boys the Vikings had only lost one game, and that was to the Knights 20 to nothing. He warned them not to be over confident, or to overlook their opponent. He knew it would be a very tight game.

Kevin wasn't worried though. His confidence was soaring. Whether the adults knew it or not, the Oilers had quietly become a team. Even though there had been adversity, it had only served to strengthen their team unity.

By now everyone on the team knew about the red truck, and the hate mail. Most of the boys did not understand it. A few were curious, especially Kevin.

Since the day Charles Taylor and his schoolmates entered Kevin's world, Kevin had questions—lots of them. And he was bound and determined to get the answers.

Gone were many of his preconceived fears and notions about black people. For now, he was just curious—he and Larry had a plan.

That afternoon, after practice concluded, Kevin decided to ride his bike home with the rest of the boys instead of catching a ride with his father.

Bill told him, "Suit yourself."

He then got in his truck, and drove home.

As Charles and Thomas walked off the practice field, Samuel and Carl took off their shoulder pads and followed them. Kevin and Larry hopped on their bikes and caught up. Randy caught up too. He straddled his bike, and walked along beside them. Paul joined them too.

As they walked across an empty field, and onto the sidewalk beside a neighborhood street, one would have thought, they were an odd-looking gang—if it weren't for their uniforms.

As they approached the first cross street, Paul left them. "See you guys tomorrow," he said. The boys all waived, and said goodbye.

After walking a few more blocks, the boys decided to take a short cut across a vacant field. Up ahead was Market Street. Across Market Street, was Colored Town. Kevin looked at Larry. Larry knew what was coming.

Kevin looked at Charles. "Where do you live, anyway?"

Charles gave Kevin a wry grin. "In the 'ville, on Carver Boulevard."

Kevin smiled.

As they continued walking, it became obvious to Randy that Kevin and Larry had an agenda. They were clearly going the wrong way. After awhile, Randy stopped. Kevin and Larry continued walking, straddling their bikes.

After a few moments, Kevin noticed Randy was no longer with them. He stopped and looked back over his shoulder. Randy stood frozen in the field like a rabbit caught in the headlights. Kevin looked over at Larry, shook his head, rolled his eyes, and then rode back alone to Randy.

The rest of the boys stopped, and looked back.

Kevin faced Randy and gestured to Market Street. "Com'on man, let's go," Kevin said.

Randy looked uneasy. "I can't."

Kevin looked impatient. "Why not?"

Randy hedged, "I just can't."

Kevin shook his head, "Okay, what ever."

Kevin turned his bike around, and began to ride back to the other boys. They were waiting at the edge of the street.

Randy called out after him, pleading with him in a low voice. "You can't go over there."

Kevin stopped and turned around. "Why not?"

Randy finally fessed up. "My dad says it's too dangerous."

Kevin looked incredulous. "Com'on?"

Randy looked serious. "It is."

After a moment, Randy explained. "My uncle works over there. He says it's not a good idea to be there after dark."

Kevin shrugged his shoulders. "It's not dark."

Randy looked at Kevin with fear in his eyes, and an emphasis in his voice. "It *will* be."

Kevin walked his bike a few steps toward him. "Look, all we're gonna do is see where they live. We'll be back before it gets dark."

Up ahead, Charles and company were beginning to look a little impatient.

Randy still hedged. "I don't know. I heard the last guy that got caught over there got both his arms and legs broke."

Kevin almost laughed. "Get outta here, that ain't true. I think you're just scared."

Randy stiffened. "No I'm not."

Kevin looked impatient. "Well then com'on."

Randy finally gave in and followed him.

At the edge of the Market Street, the boys waited until the traffic subsided. They made their way across to the other side. A couple of blocks later, Kevin, Randy and Larry entered the world where Charles and his friends lived.

The streets were clean, but the neighborhood seemed very poor. Many of the houses were small or run down. Kevin had never seen such squalor before.

As the rest of the boys walked and rode on ahead, Kevin stopped and soaked it all in.

Up ahead, Larry slowed down, and motioned for Kevin to catch up.

"Com'on, man!" Larry said.

Kevin looked at him. "Yeah, I'm comin'" he said. Kevin hurried and caught up with his friends.

That evening, as Kevin played with Charles and his little brothers in their front yard, he thought how lucky he was. He had everything compared to them. He was glad that he wasn't in their shoes.

But in a strange way, he admired them. Their hardship had made them strong. He admired their strength of will. And he wondered—oh how he wondered—he wondered what it would be like—to be black.

As evening came and went, and it began to get dark, Kevin suddenly realized he had not even called home. He knew his mom would be worried, not knowing where he was. He asked if he could make a call, but the Taylor's didn't have a phone.

How could they not have a phone? he thought. *Something just wasn't right.*

As the sun set, and the dusk settled in, Kevin looked at the darkening sky and remembered Randy's words. Larry had long since gone home. Randy had too. Kevin looked around, and then at Charles.

"I better get goin,' Kevin said.

Charles nodded. "All right."

Kevin walked over to his bike, and got on. "See ya tomorrow," Kevin added.

"Yeah, see ya," Charles replied as he watched Kevin ride away.

As Kevin rode down the street, he thought about what Randy had said. After all, the dark and unfamiliar neighborhoods did seem a little spooky. There was the sound of a hoot owl screeching in the trees. Kevin decided to pedal a little faster. Up ahead were the railroad tracks, and beyond them, was Market Street.

Maybe Randy's uncle was right, he thought. He wasn't sure, so he rose up off his seat and peddled a little harder.

Ten minutes later, he made it. He rode his bicycle up the sidewalk, and ditched it in the front yard, laying it on its side. The porch light was on.

He walked to the front door, and opened it. With his shoulder pads and helmet in his hand, he walked into the living room. Rebecca was sitting on the living room floor in her pajamas. She was watching *Underdog* on television.

"Never fear, Underdog is here," the cartoon character said.

What was she still doing up, he wondered. She looked up at him. Kevin put his finger to his mouth, and set his shoulder pads and helmet quietly onto the floor.

As he did, Mary entered the living room from the kitchen, and slammed her hands onto her hips. "Where have you been young man?"

Kevin was busted and he knew it. Rebecca tilted her blonde head to the side and smiled.

Mary continued. "Your father and I have been looking all over for you!"

"I was at Charles' house," Kevin answered.

Mary looked at the clock on the wall. "Until 7:30?"

Kevin looked contrite. "I lost track of time. We were havin' fun."

Mary was still angry. "You at least could have called?"

"They don't have a phone," Kevin explained.

Mary looked at her son. She didn't seem quite as angry anymore. "Go on and get washed up—I saved some supper for you."

Kevin patted his stomach. "I already ate."

Mary frowned.

Kevin quickly retreated. "But I could eat again."

That night, at about ten o'clock, Bill and Mary sat at the kitchen table, and discussed Kevin's tardiness. Mary clutched another piece of hate mail. She had already suggested they shouldn't let Kevin venture beyond Market Street anymore.

Bill had disagreed. He said that would be hypocritical.

Mary agreed, but said it would just be prudent, and besides that, "He shouldn't be out after dark." She added, "It just worries me, that's all."

Bill maintained his principle. "Well, I agree he shouldn't have stayed out so late, but he stays out until dark just about every night—and I'm sure not going to tell him he can't go over there to play."

Mary extended the letter to Bill. He reached over and took it from her hand. He looked at it, angrily wadded it up into a little ball, and threw it hard into the trashcan.

He pointed at Market Street. "Besides, it isn't that side of Market Street I'd be worried about!"

But Mary was not convinced. To her it didn't matter where the letters, and the intimidation, were coming from. If Kevin went over to that side of Market Street, he was likely to attract attention.

She told him so.

Bill was resolute, and reasoned, "Don't you think they would look out for him? Sure they would. Just like you would look out for Charles."

Mary seemed to agree.

"Then what's the big deal?" Bill added. "We can't live in fear."

But to Mary it *was* a big deal. She knew deep down inside it was a concern to Bill, too. Nevertheless, she decided not to press the point. She also knew Bill was a principled man— something she greatly admired in him. She had fully supported his decision to integrate the team. In fact, she had encouraged it.

Mary looked Bill in the eye. "You know what?" she said.

"What?" Bill replied.

"I love you," Mary said, confirming the look in her eye.

She reached out and gave Bill a hug. Bill kissed her on the cheek, and then looked back at her.

"It'll be ok, I know it. Now com'on, lets go to bed. It's getting late."

The following morning, Bill and Kevin sat at the kitchen table and ate breakfast together. It was Bill's day off. Mary sat at the head of the table drinking a cup of coffee, and watched them eat. Bill took a bite and chewed.

"Dale said he heard Darrell was at one of our games. Did you see him?"

Mary grimaced at his bad manners, and shook her head. "Huh uh, why would he go to our game?"

Kevin dug at his plate, "Maybe the slime-ball is gettin' worried."

Bill looked at Kevin, and gave him *the* look, "Watch your mouth."

Kevin frowned a little, and dug at his plate.

Bill looked back at Mary. "They play the Jets tonight. He was probably scouting them—or us. We're the only two unbeaten teams left. Dale says nobody has even scored on 'em yet."

Mary looked mildly impressed.

Bill swallowed. "I think I'll stick around after the game tonight, and check 'em out."

Kevin looked up, hopeful. "Can I stay too?"

Bill shook his head. "I don't think so son, it is a school night."

The clock on the kitchen wall showed eight o'clock. Bill looked up at it. "Speaking of school, you better hurry up, or you're going to be late."

Kevin looked at the clock, and took a bite. Bill looked at Mary, and grinned. Mary smiled, and sipped at her coffee.

CHAPTER ELEVEN

It was the third week of October. And it was 15 years ago to the day that Bill and his Central High School football teammates had clinched their conference title.

It was Bill's senior year, and they had gone on to win the state championship. On that night, 15 years earlier, he had been injured. He was the starting tailback, and was on his way to a stellar year, having rushed for more than 600 yards in his first six games.

But on that night, 15 years ago, he had hurt his knee, and an unknown junior had taken his place. His name was Darrell Phipps. Instead of getting the honors he would have surely earned, Bill had to stand on the sideline, and watch the remainder of the season on a pair of wooden crutches.

He also watched as his replacement erased his name from the record books, and the minds of the community.

The season- ending injury ruined Bill's chances of a college scholarship. It was something he desperately wanted. The following year, Darrell had gone on to make All-State. He eventually ended up at the university with a full ride.

Tonight the air was cool and crisp. As the ache in his left knee reminded him of what could have been, his thoughts turned to Darrell Phipps.

The Oilers were slated for the third game. The Knights and the Jets would follow after them. As usual, Charles would put on his typical performance. Several times he broke loose for large gains.

Nevertheless, the game turned into a defensive struggle. As the Oilers left the field, the scoreboard showed the final score. Oilers eight, Vikings six.

The Oilers remained undefeated.

As Bill and his team left the field that evening, Darrell and the Knights were taking it. The two coaches crossed paths. Bill spoke up first.

"Darrell, how ya doin'?"

Bill extended his hand and Darrell shook it.

"Good. Hey, I hear you all are doin' pretty good yourselves."

Bill nodded, and then Darrell pointed at the scoreboard. "What's that make ya now?"

Bill knew he knew, but he told him anyhow. "Six and zero."

Darrell smiled.

He looked as cocky as ever. "Yeah, us too—after tonight. Well, I better get out there."

Bill nodded. Darrell jabbed at him. "See ya next week."

Bill looked uncomfortable. "Yeah, see ya."

As Bill exited the field, he walked over to Mary. She was waiting for him. Kevin and Rebecca were walking ahead. "I'll see ya in a bit," Bill said. He kissed Mary on the cheek.

As Mary left, Bill made his way over to the stands. The parents and followers of the Knights already occupied many of the seats. As Bill ascended the steps, and walked to the other side, he thought he recognized several people, including Jack Simpson and Frank Felcher. Bill looked at Frank like, *don't I know you?* Frank lowered his eyes and nervously picked at a bag of popcorn. He was stone faced. Bill just shook it off, and walked on by.

As Bill made his way to the top of the bleachers, Frank looked back over his shoulder, and watched him ascend the steps. Bill sat down.

On the field, as the game began, the Knights took control. Lining up over the ball, their quarterback—Brad Phipps—took the snap, and dropped back to pass. Downfield, he quickly spotted a receiver, and threw it right to him.

Catching the ball, the receiver ran an additional 10 yards before he was tackled. So it went. The Knights completely dominated the game.

By half time, the scoreboard showed the Knights ahead 34 to nothing. They were destroying the Jets. Roger was right, they looked big for a fifth- and sixth-grade team. And unlike their opponent's sidelines, they had plenty of extras.

As the second half began, the Knights poured it on—scoring two quick touchdowns. Bill looked at the scoreboard. It read 48 to zip. Bill had seen enough. He got up, and made his way down the stands. As he neared the bottom, Frank caught his attention.

"How 'bout them Knights?"

Bill turned to the voice to acknowledge him.

"Yeah, how 'bout 'em."

Bill then stepped onto the grass, and walked away. As he got out of hearing range, Frank muttered, "Yeah, Billy Boy, it's gonna take more than a few niggers to beat us." He jabbed Jack in the arm with his elbow. Both men laughed in agreement.

The next morning, Bill and Dale were busy at work observing and recording pressure levels on various gauges. It was tedious work, but very important. The refinery turned crude oil into gasoline.

The process was meticulous. The temperatures and pressures had to be perfect. And both Bill and Dale took pride in their jobs. It may not have paid well, but to them it was important work.

The two men stood side by side. They were both wearing hard hats. Bill cupped his hand over one of the gauges, blocking the glare of the sun. "One-sixty at 20," he said. Dale nodded, and wrote the figures down on his clipboard.

"I'm tellin' ya it wasn't even close," Bill added. "I left in the middle of the third quarter, no tellin' how bad they beat 'em."

Dale eyed his clipboard as he jotted down some information.

"It couldn't have been that bad," Dale replied.

"Well it was. They're everything Ted said they were—and more. They're like a high- pressure machine."

Bill tapped a pressure gauge, as if to make a point. The needle was nearly pegged to the right.

Bill tapped at it again. "And they don't back off," he added. Bill stepped away, and walked to the next set of gauges.

Dale followed him. "Don't tell me Mr. Optimistic has given up already?"

Bill shook his head. "I'm just being *realistic*, that's all."

Dale wrote down some information from one of the gauges, and the two men moved on down the line.

Monday morning Bill awoke early, assembled his notes on the kitchen table, and began to formulate his game plan for Thursday night. All season long, he had kept a detailed journal of every game. In it, he wrote what had worked—and what had not.

Watching the Knights systematically dismantle the Jets on Thursday night, Bill had seen no weakness. In their first six games, the Knights, according to league records, had scored 302 points. It was the most of any team in league history.

What was more amazing was the fact their opponents had scored zero. In contrast, the Oilers had out scored their opponents 134 to 42.

On paper, the Oilers were outmatched.

If the Oilers were to pull off the upset, Bill reasoned, it would start with solid defense. They had played well together all year long, with few exceptions. Even with the addition of the new kids, he knew it would be a challenge.

On offense, Bill was even more concerned. He knew the Knights would key on Charles. Or at least, that was what he would do if he were in Darrell's shoes.

In fact, Charles prowess was already well- known throughout the league. One coach was so impressed; he had actually called Bill, and asked him to give his regards to Number 24.

Another had commented Charles may have been the best athlete ever to play in the league—and that was saying a lot. Many kids had gone on to become high school stars, and not a few had excelled at the college level.

Bill summarized his thoughts. He felt if they were to have a chance against the Knights, he would have to rely on the defense—and the element of surprise.

As Bill arrived at work that morning, he, Dale and Roger were assigned to the tanks. The task was simple enough, but very tiring. By the end of the shift, the three men had climbed up virtually every ladder and checked every gauge. They had carefully recorded the pressure levels to pass on to the next shift.

As the whistle blew, and the shift ended, Bill and Dale exited gate number Five. They waved goodbye to the guard, and headed straight for the practice field.

Bill asked the boys to make a commitment that week to show up a little earlier for practice. They did, every last one of them. By 3:45, all 28 United Oil Workers Union Oilers were on the field, ready for practice to begin.

As the Oilers worked that afternoon, Bill and Dale concentrated on the defense, and stressed the fundamentals.

"Put your hat on the ball, get your head across—drive with your hips," Bill exhorted.

Bill nit picked each mistake. When Carl over ran the ball, Bill became very animated.

"Break down, son—get under control!" Bill demonstrated what he meant.

Carl seemed to have understood. He nodded. Bill tapped him on the top of the helmet, and sent him back onto the field.

Not far from where the Oilers were practicing, but a world apart, Darrell was also preparing for the game. A successful car dealer by day, Darrell was also a shrewd businessman.

He, too, had learned to never leave anything to chance. But at the moment, Darrell had other concerns, as he leaned back in his comfortable chair. He stuck his feet on top of his desk, and put the phone up to his ear. On the wall behind him were many framed certificates, awards, and diplomas. On his bookshelf there were several championship trophies.

"Jack, Darrell Phipps, How ya doin'? Good, listen. I got a question for ya. I heard a nasty rumor the other day. I was wonderin' if you might check it out for me?"

Later that evening, on their own practice field, the McKinley Knights gathered around their coach. Darrell looked intense as he surveyed his troops.

His speech was short and to the point. "Listen up! We've got one game left! There is only one team that stands between us and the city championship. The Oilers."

The Knights began to boo and hiss. Darrell waited for a moment, then raised his hands and quieted them down.

"Now I'm not going to try to put the fear in ya, because it probably wouldn't do me any good. There's no reason why you shouldn't beat these guys. They've had a lot of close games. Last week they only beat the Vikings eight to six. We beat 'em 20 to nothing. We've scouted them well—and come game time, we'll be prepared. So let's have a good week of practice, and then kick some butt on Thursday night!"

The Knights began to hoop and holler—they heartily agreed. Darrell smiled and added, "Offense with Coach Baker, defense, follow me."

As the team separated into two groups, Coach Phipps took the defense to the other end of the practice field, where they reassembled and gathered around him.

"Now listen up!" Darrell said. "There is only one kid that we have to worry about." Darrell then pulled out an Oilers jersey with the number 24. Inside the collar was the name C. TAYLOR written in black ink.

"He's quick as lightning, and black as night. And he's got plenty of moves. But come Thursday night, we're gonna hit him, hit him hard—and then we're gonna tell him about it!"

Once again the troops were riled.

Darrell continued. "Nobody has scored on us all year, and I like it that way. So this is what we're gonna do. Kenny—Scott—

—Lance! Wherever he goes, *you go.* I want you to shadow him, and I want you to hit him every chance you get."

Darrell then tossed the jersey on the ground, and looked at the boys. "Any questions? All right let's get after it!"

By Wednesday night, Bill thought he had done everything he could do. Earlier in the day at their final practice, he had put in a few new plays, including one trick play, which he thought he might use—if the situation was right.

He called it, "The Sleeper."

Later that evening, as Bill sat alone at the kitchen table drinking a glass of milk, he looked over his notes one last time. He looked tired. His eyes were red. He rubbed them.

The clock on the wall showed 10 o'clock. Bill looked up at it as Mary entered the kitchen in her nightgown. Bill smiled at her. Mary smiled back. She stepped behind him, and bent over and gave him a gentle kiss on his forehead.

"I'm going to bed," she said.

Bill looked up. "I'll be there in a minute, honey."

After a few minutes, Bill straightened up the notes, and placed them on the counter, near his lunch pail. He turned off the light, and walked across the living room to the hallway. As he walked by Kevin's room, he noticed Kevin's light was still on.

The light was coming from underneath the door. Bill quietly opened the door, and looked in.

Kevin was sitting on the edge of his bed looking out the window. On the bed were a few play sheets he had been studying.

"What are you still doin' up?" Bill asked.

Kevin glanced back at his father. "I couldn't sleep."

Bill entered the room. He pulled out a chair from the desk, and straddled it backwards.

"You looked like you were doin' some heavy thinkin'," he said.

Kevin looked at his father and then out the window again.

"Remember the other day, when me and Randy followed Charles and Thomas home?" Kevin looked back at Bill.

Bill nodded, "Yeah?"

Kevin looked back out the window, and continued, "How come white folks aren't allowed over there?"

Bill inhaled, exhaled softly, and reflected for a moment. "Who told you that?"

Kevin looked back at Bill. "Randy. He said his dad told him to stay away from there."

Bill leaned forward, "Then he better do what his dad says."

Kevin cocked his head to the side, "How come you let me go over there?"

Bill seemed a little uncomfortable. "You sure do ask a lotta questions."

Kevin persisted, "Well, why do ya?"

Bill inhaled and exhaled slowly again. "You know how there were rest rooms that used to say, "colored" and "white?" How everything was always separated? Well, those things are changing.

"Now the rest rooms just say gentlemen and ladies. They aren't separated any more." Bill explained.

"But they still got their own school," Kevin said.

Bill agreed. "Yeah, but even that is changing. Pretty soon that won't be separated either."

Kevin thought for a moment, and then looked back out the window. His reflection in the glass revealed the depth of his thought.

"You know, those people are poor," he said.

Bill chuckled, "Kinda like us, huh?"

But Kevin shook his head hard, "No. I mean *really* poor." Kevin looked back to his father. "Is that gonna change too?"

Bill softly exhaled. "I don't know son. I can't answer that one. Now you get some sleep, you got a big day ahead of you tomorrow."

Bill stood up and pushed the chair back. Kevin grabbed the play sheets, and set them beside the bed. Bill opened the door, and then looked back at his son. "Goodnight."

Kevin gently nodded, "'night."

Bill turned off the light, and closed the door.

As Kevin laid his head on the pillow that night, his thoughts once again turned to the championship trophy. As he closed his eyes, and fell asleep—he dreamed of winning it.

Down the hall, as Bill lay down next to Mary that evening, his mind raced. Mary tried her best to sleep. Bill was wide-awake. Lying on his back, with his hands behind his head and elbows sticking out, Bill looked at the ceiling as if he were trying to memorize it.

Finally, he couldn't help it, and broke the silence. "You know, I've been thinkin'. If we win tomorrow, we'll have done somethin' that no one has been able to do for years."

Mary rolled over to him.

Her voice was sleepy. "Oh yeah? What's that?"

Bill's eyes were almost burning a hole in the ceiling. "Beat Darrell Phipps. Ever since I've known him, he's always done better than me—better in school, football, *everything*. He's even good lookin'."

"I mean look at him. He's got a good job, lives in a nice house." Bill paused for a second, and looked at Mary. "He seems like he's got everything."

Mary looked back at him. "Do I detect a little bit of envy? Look, money's not everything. You definitely can't measure success by it. Look at us—we may not have a lot, but we're happy. We got good kids, a house, and nice neighbors. You got a good job."

Mary's facial expression changed to one of contempt. She turned back over on her other side, and attempted to get comfortable. "Besides, I bet Darrell Phipps isn't so good lookin' on the inside."

Bill sighed. "Yeah? Maybe you're right. I never really looked at it like that."

The following morning, on game day, Darrell was back at his desk doing paperwork. On his desk, was a picture of his wife and kids. Darrell glanced at it, as in the doorway a very pretty young secretary appeared.

"Darrell, Jack Simpson is on line one."

Darrell looked up. "Thanks."

As she left, he watched the sway of her hips. He picked up the phone and punched a button.

"This is Darrell. Jack! How ya doin'? Well, what'd ya find out? Uh huh. Well that's good to know. No I'm not worried. Let's just call it insurance. You are in the insurance business." Darrell laughed. "Yeah. Nah, I don't think it's gonna matter. All right, see ya tonight. Uh huh, bye bye."

Darrell hung up the phone, and began twirling a pencil between his fingers. He looked up at the shelf at the championship trophies. There was room for one more.

CHAPTER TWELVE

At precisely 3 o'clock, on Thursday afternoon in late October, the steam whistle blew at the refinery. In less then five hours, Bill and his Oilers would take the field.

As he and Dale exited the gate and headed for their trucks, there was only one thing on Bill's mind; the McKinley Knights.

He was already nervous. It showed in his face. It was game day. He was always nervous on game day. But today, it was worse.

As Bill got in his truck, the coolness of the air felt refreshing to his lungs. *It was perfect weather for football*, he thought. Arriving home that afternoon, he avoided the mail, and attempted to eat, but he couldn't, there were just too many butterflies in his stomach.

By 7:20 PM, Bill was ready. He and Kevin gathered up the equipment and tossed it into the back of the truck. Mary and

Rebecca got in. Bill looked at Kevin and softly winked, "Lets go sport." Kevin smiled and hopped inside. Bill got in too and they drove to PAL field. It was only a 10-minute drive.

When they arrived, the prior game was in the middle the third quarter. The Vikings were whipping the Jets 18 to 6.

Most, if not all, the Oilers players had already arrived. The boys helped Bill get the balls and equipment from the back of his truck and began to warm up in the adjacent lot.

Bill stood nearby and watched as Kevin threw one tight spiral after another. Thomas caught every one. Kevin's arm seemed to be getting stronger and stronger. *They just might need it*, Bill thought.

Fifteen minutes later, the game between the Vikings and Jets concluded. Bill and Dale watched the final seconds of the clock tick off. They sent the boys onto the field, and lined them up for their pre-game drills.

At about eight o'clock—just before game time—Bill pointed to the south end zone. Dale nodded and led the Oilers to the end of the field, and assembled under the goal post.

As the Oilers prepared to take their sideline, Bill was as nervous as he had ever been. His stomach was in knots. Even on his wedding night he had not been as tight as he was now—or so he thought.

Beside him, the boys were sky high. They were jumping up and down, smashing into each other's helmets. Bill hoped they would save some of that energy for the game, but by the looks of them, they were plenty ready.

The announcer welcomed the crowd to PAL field for the season's final game; there was excitement in the air. In the stands, the crowd was already in their seats.

On the Oilers side, the Oilers fans were fully integrated. They had no choice—there wasn't a seat left. There were many familiar faces, including Roger, and the Taylor's. Ed Rivers had even shown up.

On the Knight's side of the bleachers, the crowd was packed in like sardines. In the middle, sat Frank and Jack. Below the stands and on the sides, standing on the grass, there were many other people too.

The crowd was overflowing.

In the south end zone, Bill tried to calm the boys down. He took center stage. Surrounded by his Oilers, he looked at each of their faces. All eyes were fixed upon Bill. He took a deep breath and exhaled.

In the other end zone were their opponents, the McKinley Knights. Seas of gold helmets were bobbing up and down. Under the lights, their helmets seemed to glow as if they were on fire.

In the press box, the announcer was about to announce them to the crowd. As he did, Bill motioned for his boys to take a knee. In the stands, there was a loud cheer, and with a rush, the Knights took the field.

They were an impressive sight.

"Listen up!" Bill said, as he attempted to coax their attention away from their opponents. "Tonight is very important. If you win, they'll call you champions, if you don't, well, nobody expected ya to. But no matter what happens, I want you all to know how very proud I am of you. All of you."

Bill looked at Kevin, then at Charles, Larry, and Carl. "Now we got this far by being a team. Let's not forget that. All I ask is that you give me 110%."

Beside Bill, Dale looked intense. The boys looked ready. "All right, everybody on your feet!"

As the announcer announced the Oilers, the boys let out a loud yell, and rushed onto the field.

Bill smiled, shook his head at Dale, and inhaled deeply. "You ready?"

Dale nodded. He could barely breathe himself.

As Bill and Dale jogged to their sideline, the boys re-assembled. Two referees came onto the field. Bill looked around and spotted Charles.

"Charles!"

Charles looked at Bill. "Yes sir?"

Bill looked him in the eye. "You're team captain tonight. You and Larry."

Charles eyes lit up. "Yes sir!"

The Oilers gathered around Charles and Larry, and put their hands into the circle. In unison, they began to let out their voices, "Ooooooooo."

After about five seconds their voices formed a loud crescendo, "*Oilers!*" The boys dispersed along their sideline.

On the opposite side of the field the Knights were ready, too. Two representatives walked to midfield, they looked very big.

Charles and Larry approached them, meeting them at the center. The officials moved them to opposite sides of the field to face each other.

The players shook hands. The Oilers were the visiting team.

The head official spoke up. "Who's gonna make the call?"

Charles nudged Larry. "Go ahead."

Larry shook his head. "No, you do it."

The official tossed the coin into the air. As it flipped, Charles watched it, and then called it. "Heads!"

The coin hit the turf heads side up.

The referee looked at the Oilers sideline. "The Oilers win the toss," he said.

The official asked Charles, "Do you want to kick or receive?"

Charles looked at Bill, and replied, "We'll defer 'til the second half."

The official nodded. "All right."

He signaled to the crowd the Knights would receive, and the Oilers would kick.

As both teams lined up for the opening kickoff, the Knights, looked very confident. They were all big kids.

On the Oilers sideline, the players were wide- eyed. They looked a little intimidated.

The Oilers kicker walked out to the 30-yard line, and placed the ball on the tee. He waited for the referee's signal, and on the whistle, he ran at the ball and booted it end over end downfield.

The ball sailed to the 20-yard line of the Knights. The Knight receiver caught it in the air, and sprinted upfield. Darting between two Oilers defenders, he returned it to the 35-yard line where Carl promptly decked him.

The sound of the popping pads filled the air. It was a good hit.

As the Knights filed along the line of scrimmage for their first play, the Oilers scrambled to get in position.

The Knights offensive line was massive. They outweighed the Oilers by 20 pounds each. Brad Phipps bent under his center. His eyes were full of confidence. He barked out his signals. The line raised up, and then lowered simultaneously into a set position. It looked impressive. As the ball was snapped, Brad turned and handed it to a running back. He ran it straight up the middle. The hole was huge. He gained at least 10 yards.

As the whistle blew, Bill shook his head. "That hole was big enough to drive a truck through," Bill said aloud.

"Wow," Dale said.

Across the way, Darrell smiled as the chains moved downfield.

Darrell quickly sent in his next play. The Knights went to the air as Brad dropped back to pass. It seemed like he had all day. The Oilers rush was non-existent. Finally, Brad spotted a receiver downfield, and threw him a perfect spiral pass.

The receiver caught the ball and turned upfield, and then just before contact, he stepped out of bounds. The play had netted another 15 yards, and another first down.

Once again, the chains moved downfield.

A few plays later, the Knights were about to score. It had been a methodical drive. Bill could only watch as Darrell's son handed off to a running back, who then sprinted to his right— and headed for the flag.

He was too fast, and a wall of blockers cut off the Oilers pursuit. Letting up a little at the end, the Knights running back jogged untouched into the corner of the end zone. The referee blew his whistle, and raised his hands.

The Knights were on the board, and they had made it look easy too. A 45- yard drive in only five plays. Bill bit at his lower lip, and shook his head. *This could be a long night*, he thought.

On the other sideline, Darrell looked at his players, and slapped his hands. "It's about time damn it!"

As the Knights lined up for the extra point, the Oilers bench watched. The ball was snapped and placed. The Knight's kicker stepped forward, and kicked the ball squarely through the uprights. It was an impressive sight.

One Oilers player stood to his feet in obvious awe, "Man, they even *kick* their extra points!"

The scoreboard showed the results: Knights 7 Oilers 0.

After a short kick return, the Oilers offense took the field. Kevin immediately handed the football to Charles, who ran to his right. Four Knights promptly swarmed him.

Charles only managed to pick up one yard. The next two plays yielded little more, and the down marker moved to fourth down. The length of the chain showed about four yards to go.

The Oilers would have to punt.

As the punter came into the game, and the Oilers set up, the Knights sent three men deep, and prepared for the return. As the ball was snapped, the Oilers' punter kicked it high and downfield about 30 yards. It was a good punt, and the Oilers covered it well. The Knight receiver had to settle for a fair catch.

As the Knight's offense retook the field, they quickly picked up where they left off. About six plays later, early in the second quarter, they scored again. On the Oilers sideline there were nothing but looks of dejection.

It was a stark contrast to the Knights sideline. The Knights were jumping up and down, and slapping hands. In the stands, the Oilers parents looked concerned. But not the parents of the Knight's, they were chatting up a storm. Their team looked unstoppable.

When the Oilers got the ball back, Darrell poured it on, and called for a blitz, and then another. Time and again, they hit Kevin hard.

Charles faired no better. Each time he touched the ball, three or four Knights were waiting on him. And when they hit him—they hit him hard, and drove him into the ground. They were gang- tackling him, and it looked like it hurt.

On the last offensive possession of the first half, Bill decided he would try something different. So far nothing had worked. Their previous attempts to move the ball had proven unsuccessful. The Knights were blitzing on every down.

Bill sent in the play with Thomas. "Fake 33, halfback flair right."

Thomas nodded and took the play to the huddle.

As the Oilers broke their huddle, and lined up on the ball, Kevin looked at his fullback, bent under the center and began barking out his signals. "Down!" Kevin said.

Across the way a linebacker stepped in between the guard-center gap. He was going to blitz. Kevin knew it.

"Setttt," Kevin bellowed out. Kevin looked the defender in the eye. "Hut one!"

The linebacker chewed at his mouthpiece. "You're dead meat man"

Kevin's eyes widened. He finished his count. "Hut two!"

The ball was snapped. As Charles flared out to the right, Kevin turned to his left, and faked a handoff to his fullback. The linebacker met him in the backfield. As he did, Kevin pulled the ball back from the fullback's stomach and dropped back to pass. Kevin whirled around.

For the first time all night, the Knights had been caught off guard. Their linebackers had bit on the fullback dive. The over aggressive play of the Knights had worked to the Oilers advantage.

In the flat, Charles was wide open. Kevin's eyes widened as he lobbed a pass out right at him. As the ball sailed, Charles looked downfield. There was nothing but green grass in front of him. He could easily score.

But Charles had broken a cardinal rule. He had taken his eye off the ball. As he looked up, the ball hit him squarely in the chest, bounced off, and fell harmlessly to the turf.

Bill rolled his head at the missed opportunity. But what he saw next, made his blood boil.

As the ball hit the ground and rolled along the turf, one of the Knights' safeties came flying by. He slammed into Charles with all his might.

Charles head snapped back as he hit the ground hard. It was Lance Felcher, Frank's son. As Charles attempted to regain his senses, Lance stood towering over him. He looked Charles in the eye.

"Take that *nigger!*"

On the Oilers sideline, Bill was beside himself. An official had been standing right there.

"Hey! He can't do that. That's un-sportsman like conduct!"

The official looked ambivalent. Bill then stepped onto the field, reached for his back pocket and demonstrated throwing a flag.

"Where's the flag! You can't let him get away with that!"

Charles slowly got up. He seemed to wobble a little as he walked to the sideline. The referee watched him walk by, then looked at Bill and slowly turned his back on him. He then blew his whistle to resume play.

On the opposite sideline Darrell was smiling from ear to ear.

As the Knights got the ball back, the clock was winding down. Darrell decided to play it safe, and sent in a running play.

Brad handed the ball to a running back, who ran right, and then cut upfield for a five-yard gain. At a distance, on the scoreboard, the clock ticked down to zero, and the horn sounded. It was half time. The scoreboard showed the score Knights 14, Oilers nothing.

At half time, Bill addressed his players in the end zone, and attempted to encourage them. There were a lot of depressed faces. The boys looked beat.

As the clock on the scoreboard was ticking down 14...13...12...11... Bill gave them one last bit of pep. "Keep your heads up! This game ain't over with yet. You got one half of football left. Don't leave anything on the field, give it all you got, and you won't have anything to be ashamed of."

It seemed to have helped. As the horn sounded, Bill looked at Dale. Dale clapped his hands.

"Lets go guys," Dale said.

As the boys got up and followed Dale to the sideline, Bill headed for midfield, where the officials were gathered. On his way there, he grabbed Charles.

"You all right?"

Charles nodded, "Yeah."

Bill wanted to make sure. "You sure?"

Charles nodded once more. There was a spot of blood on his chin-strap. Bill glanced at it. He then let him go and continued to midfield. Once there, he conferred with the officials for a few moments. From a distance, it looked like Bill was giving them a piece of his mind. He had his hands on his hips. He raised a hand and pointed right at one of them. He then turned, ran back to the sideline.

Dale was waiting. He stepped out onto the field as Bill approached.

"Well?" Dale asked.

"I told 'em what I thought."

"And what about the play?" Dale asked.

Bill looked Dale in the eye. "I let him know we might use it."

Dale wanted to know more. "And?"

Bill put his hand on Dale's shoulder. "They said it's legal."

As Bill and Dale walked down the sideline, one of the officials walked to them. "I need a team captain."

Bill pointed to Larry. Larry followed him to midfield where one of the Knights was already waiting.

On the Oilers sideline, the receiving team huddled around Bill, and then broke out onto the field. As both teams lined up for the kickoff, Charles ran to about the 10-yard line, then stopped, and turned around.

He was alone. Bill looked at him and clapped his hands. "Com'on Charles, show 'em what you can do."

Charles looked at Bill. He looked like he had the weight of the world on his shoulders.

As the official blew his whistle, and dropped his arm, Bill watched expectantly. The kicker for the Knights slowly approached the ball, then kicked it end over end downfield.

Charles moved to his right to get under it. The ball hit him in the chest. He bobbled it momentarily, and then gained control.

As several Knights converged on him, Charles reversed direction, and broke for the far sideline. He was running right at Bill. Two Knights were in hot pursuit.

Reaching the sideline—just shy of midfield, Charles turned the corner in front of Bill. He was off balance—barely in bounds. Bill looked down at his feet. He could have swore Charles hit chalk, but he wasn't sure.

Upfield, the remaining Knights had the angle—at about their own 30-yard line—they caught up to Charles, and shoved him out of bounds.

Bill was very animated. "Atta boy Charles, now we're talkin'!"

The Oilers were moving the ball. With the down marker showing third down and three to go, Bill called for a pass. *They'll be looking for a run*, he thought. He sent the play in with Larry. Larry hustled onto the field, stepped into the huddle, and relayed the play to Kevin.

He tugged at the left side of his jersey. "Wide right, middle curl."

Kevin nodded and repeated the play. "Wide right, middle curl, on set. Ready, break!"

The Oilers broke the huddle in unison.

Stepping under his center, Kevin looked out to the right. Larry was set. Kevin looked back out over the defense and barked out his signals. "Dowwwn, set!"

Taking the snap, he rolled out to his right past his tackle. Samuel Ellis flattened the defensive end and laid on him.

Kevin looked downfield for an open receiver. No one was open. As two defenders quickly converged on him, one from the left, and one from the right, Kevin performed his patented move.

He stopped on a dime, and ducked. The defender on his left slid right over the top of him, and smashed into the defender on the right. The collision was loud. It could be heard across the field. Darrell winced, as two of his Knights hit the ground, hard.

With no one to chase him, Kevin calmly reversed direction. He spotted Larry downfield, and hit him with a perfect pass. After a small additional gain, the receiver was taken down.

On the field, Kevin was smiling ear to ear as he watched the two Knights slowly get up.

Randy looked at them. He shook his head, and laughed, "Ouch."

Randy had been there before. He congratulated Kevin with a swat to the head. "Way to go man!"

On the Oilers sideline, Bill and Dale looked rejuvenated, and the rest of the Oilers did too. On the opposite sideline, Darrell was showing the first sign of concern. The momentum had definitely shifted, and Darrell knew it.

It was now first down, on the Knights' 15- yard line. The Oilers were moving the ball. Kevin took the snap and pitched it to Charles, who ran to his left—and then cut upfield.

The crowd stood to their feet as he juked two defenders, and left them clutching for air. Only one defender now stood between him and the goal line.

It was Lance.

Charles gritted his teeth, and lowered his shoulder as if he wanted to run him over. Lance coiled for the impact and lowered his head. But instead of hitting him head- on, at the last second, Charles rose up, and spun around.

Lance got nothing but air.

Charles sidestepped him, and jogged the remaining few yards into the end zone.

On the Oilers sideline, the Oilers players were screaming for joy. In the end zone, Charles was smiling ear to ear. Back upfield, Lance was humiliated, and so was Darrell.

He stormed onto the field. There went his perfect un-scored upon season. Darrell threw down his clipboard in front of Lance and began to berate him. His voice was so loud that it seemed everyone could hear it.

"What in the hell is wrong with you!" he said. "You just let him run right by you!"

Lance looked very embarrassed. Darrell grabbed him by the facemask, and pulled him even closer. "Open your eyes for Pete's sake."

Darrell let him go, and shoved him away. He bent down, grabbed his clipboard, looked back at Lance and added, "If you can't do your job, I'll find someone who will!"

Lance sheepishly nodded. Darrell turned his back on him, and walked back to the sideline.

In the stands, Lance's father, Frank, stood up. He looked destroyed and angry.

His lip quivered. "Why that sonofa..."

Opposite Frank were several parents looking straight at him. Frank realized where he was, and attempted to control his tongue. He looked at Jack, and pointed at the field.

"He can't talk to him like that!" Frank was so mad, he was shaking like a leaf. "Did you see that? Did you see what he did?"

He lowered his voice, and muttered, "Why nobody should talk to a kid like that! Nobody!"

CHAPTER THIRTEEN

As Bill looked at the scoreboard, his confidence grew. On the field, the Knights had the ball, and the Oilers defense looked pumped up.

As Brad Phipps lined up under center and took the snap, it was obvious the momentum had changed. Carl ripped through the line, and nailed a Knight running back for a two-yard loss.

The Knights were stymied. The down marker changed to fourth down. They would have to punt.

After returning the ball for little gain, the Oilers offense retook the field. The ball was on the Oilers 30- yard line. Kevin stepped under center, took the snap, and handed off to Charles. He quickly picked up four yards. Two plays later, the chains moved downfield. It was first down. Bill sent in another play.

Kevin took the snap and dropped back to pass. Once again, Samuel Ellis flattened the rushing End and laid on him. Downfield and to his left, Kevin spotted Paul. He was wide open. He delivered him the ball for another first down. On the Knight sideline, Darrell looked worried. He looked at the scoreboard, the clock was ticking down.

As the Oilers began to huddle, an official blew his whistle—signifying the end of the third quarter. The final eight minutes were put on the clock. The scoreboard now read, Knights 14, Oilers 6.

Kevin trotted to the sideline. Bill waited. As Kevin approached, Bill looked him in the eye.

"You all right?" he asked.

Kevin nodded. "Yeah."

Bill swatted him on the helmet. "All right, we're gonna run a reverse. Fake the dive, then give it to Thomas comin' around. Twenty-eight reverse right, on one."

Kevin looked unsure. "What if he runs me over like he did the last time?"

Bill looked resolute. "Hey! Who's the coach here? Just run the play!"

Kevin quickly agreed. "Twenty-eight reverse right, on one."

Bill nodded, and Kevin returned to the field.

As the official blew his whistle, the Oilers broke their huddle. Kevin stepped under center, and began to bark out the signals. "Down! Settt. Hut one."

The ball was snapped. Kevin quickly faked the ball to the fullback, who dove into the line.

Hiding the ball on his back hip, Kevin sprinted to his left. At the last second he reached back and handed it to Thomas—coming at him on the reverse.

It worked perfectly.

Thomas sprinted for the right side line. The Knights were caught off guard. The crowd in the stands stood to its feet—collectively "oooooing."

As Thomas turned upfield, he sprinted down the sideline, pumping his knees as hard as he could. He only had one man to beat. It was the safety, Lance.

Out of nowhere, Charles appeared with fire in his eyes.

Lance never saw him.

Charles lowered his head—and sent him reeling with a crunching block.

Thomas' eyes opened wide. He had nothing but green grass in front of him. A few moments later, he arrived untouched in the end zone. A melee promptly ensued. It seemed like the entire Oilers team was in the end zone, piling on Thomas.

All, except for Charles, who stood towering over his conquest—who looked a bit blurry- eyed.

"Don't you ever call me *that name* again," Charles scolded. Lance looked up—he seemed agreeable.

The Oilers were still celebrating in the end zone. Charles joined them. But Bill, sensing the need of the moment, stepped onto the field.

"Kevin! Come here!"

Kevin was very excited, but regained his composure, and ran over to his father. Bill smiled. The scoreboard read, Knights 14, Oilers 12.

Bill looked at it, and then looked back at Kevin. "We need two. Fake the dive left, and hit Charles on the run pass option, all right?"

Kevin nodded.

Bill repeated the play. "Fake 33 left, run pass option right, and tell Charles to get open."

Kevin repeated it back. Bill nodded. Kevin returned to the field.

Bill yelled out after him, "On one!"

Kevin seemed to have heard.

With the conversion attempt on the line, Kevin squatted under his center, took the snap, and executed the play. He faked the handoff into the line, reversed direction, and rolled out to his right.

As a defender crossed the line, Charles sprinted past him, and then bent to the right. He was wide open.

Kevin was about to be hit. He lofted the ball over the oncoming defender right to Charles. The ball hit him squarely in the chest, and fell to the ground. The conversion failed.

Charles was dejected. The Knights were screaming with glee. Kevin gritted his teeth, looked at Charles and tried his best not to make him feel bad. Charles walked off the field with his head down low. The scoreboard still read Knights 14, Oilers 12.

Time was running out. The clock showed less than two minutes to go—and the Knights had the ball. It was second down. As the clock ticked away, Charles sat alone on the bench, with his head buried in his hands.

On the field, the quarterback for the Knights took the snap and handed the ball off to a running back who was tackled for little gain. On the Knight sideline Darrell smiled broadly. His assistant coaches were also smiling as they chatted with each other. Bill immediately called time out and stopped the clock. An official walked to the sideline to talk to him.

"That's your last time out, coach," he said. Bill nodded.

As play resumed, the quarterback for the Knights took the snap, and fell to a knee. The clock continued to tick down. At about 20 seconds, the official blew his whistle and stopped the clock.

He penalized the Knights for delay of game, and their punter came onto the field. On the Oilers sideline, Bill looked for Charles, and found him.

"Charles."

Charles stood up, helmet in hand.

"Return the punt."

Charles put on his helmet, and sprinted onto the field.

As the Oilers broke the huddle, Charles ran downfield about 30 yards, and turned around. He glanced at the clock. There were only 20 seconds left. Upfield, the Knights broke their huddle, and lined up over the ball. The Oilers lined up 10 men on the line of scrimmage in order to try to block the punt.

As the ball was snapped, the punter received it cleanly and quickly kicked a line drive. It bounced once, twice. Charles scooped it up and ran to his left, but there were too many defenders.

He stopped, reversed his direction, and ran to the right. Again, there were too many Knights.

He tried to turn upfield, but there was nowhere to go. He sprinted for the sideline—just to get out of bounds. The whistle blew. The clock showed 11 seconds left. Bill grabbed Charles as he stepped back onto the field.

Kevin put on his helmet and ran to the huddle.

Bill called out after him, "Kevin!"

Kevin stopped and looked back at his father. Bill locked him in his gaze. "We're gonna run the SLEEPER."

Kevin looked puzzled. "Who's the sleeper?"

Bill nodded at Charles. Kevin looked uneasy. "Are you sure?"

Bill was emphatic. "Yes!"

Kevin wagged his head. "All right." He began to run to the huddle.

An official approached the sideline. Bill looked at him. "We're gonna run it now."

The official looked at Charles, and then at his feet. He was barely in bounds, standing at the line of scrimmage facing Bill. The official nodded, and turned back to the field of play.

Charles looked scared. Bill attempted to be reassuring. "This is what we're gonna do. When I tell you to take off, you run down the side line about 20 yards. *Stay in bounds!* Kevin is gonna throw you the ball."

Charles began to shake his head.

"You can do it. Keep your eye on the ball and watch it in."

On the field Kevin broke the huddle with 10 players. Nobody noticed the man missing. Kevin stood under center and glanced at the sideline. Nobody had come out to cover Charles.

Bill looked Charles in the eye one more time. "Are you ready?" Charles looked petrified. The ball was snapped. Kevin began to roll out to the sideline.

Bill looked intense. *"Go!"*

Charles took off. About 20 yards downfield, he looked back for the ball. Kevin was under pressure, he squared his shoulders on a dead run as three defenders converged on him.

The secondary of the Knights were motionless. They couldn't see a receiver.

Kevin heaved the ball with all his might. The Knights' safety finally spotted Charles. He was wide open. He sprinted at him. As the ball sailed through the air—the safety converged.

For a brief moment time seemed to slow down. Charles' eyes grew as big as saucers.

The ball hit him in the chest.

Like a bar of soap, it squirted out of his hands and onto the top of his shoulder pad. With one hand, Charles reached up, and pulled it in.

Suddenly, it seemed everything was back to real time. The safety lowered his head to hit Charles, but Charles shifted his hips—and avoided him like a bullfighter in a ring.

He then sprinted downfield for the end zone. The final horn sounded as he crossed the line.

Pandemonium ensued. The Knights were in shock. Darrell couldn't believe it. He cursed the night air. Then, in a fit of rage, he slung his clipboard like a Frisbee at his team's bench. Upon impact, it seemed to shatter into a thousand pieces.

Back in the end zone, the Oilers were extremely jubilant. The entire team was piling on Charles.

If you've have ever been on the bottom of the pile before, then you could have truly appreciated what happened next— after quite a bit of celebration, Charles was hoisted high into the air on top of his teammates' shoulders. From on high he looked at his father—who was now standing on the sideline.

Mr.Taylor smiled proudly from ear to ear.

In the stands there was shock and disbelief, mixed with celebration The parents of the Oilers were exchanging hugs and handshakes.

On the Oilers sideline, Bill had been left alone. He was staring across the field. He made eye contact with Darrell. Darrell shook his head in disbelief.

The Oilers were the new city champions.

CHAPTER FOURTEEN

At one end of the field under the goal posts, the United Oil Workers Union Oilers assembled, and posed for a team picture. Sitting in the front row was Charles Taylor proudly holding the championship trophy.

Bill and Dale stood on opposite ends of the back row. The kids were beaming with big smiles, as the camera flashed. Two gentlemen, one wearing a brown suit, the other gray, walked to Bill and Dale as the boys began to disperse.

One of the men reached out and shook Bill's hand. "Once again, congratulations on a fine season," he said.

Bill nodded. "Thanks."

The official shook Dale's hand. "Congratulations."

"Thanks," Dale replied.

The two officials exited to the right, and walked off the field. Near the exit gate, Darrell stood by waiting.

As the two PAL officials walked by, he stopped them. And thus they began a long conversation. After a few minutes, one of the officials began walking back to Dale. Dale noticed him, took his leave of Bill, and walked out to meet him.

As Dale and the PAL official talked, Bill walked out to the middle of the field to savor the moment. As he was walking, a reporter for the local paper followed him.

"Excuse me, Mr. Campbell."

Bill stopped, and turned around. "Yes?"

The reporter pulled out a notepad. "I'm with the Daily Eagle. I wanted to congratulate you on your win tonight, that was an incredible game. Did you know they hadn't lost a game in three years?"

Bill nodded.

The reporter continued, "I was wondering if I could ask you a few questions."

Bill nodded. "Sure."

The reporter put his pencil to the pad. "What do you call that play you used there at the end?"

Bill smiled, "It's called The Sleeper."

The reporter shook his head, and wrote it down. "That was some play. To what do you attribute your success this season?"

Bill thought for a moment, looked at the scoreboard and smiled, "A low turnout."

The reporter wrote the reply down, and then looked up confused. "A what?"

Bill shook his head, "Uhhh, never mind that, that would be kind of hard to explain."

The reporter nodded, but he was still obviously confused. "You know that it is customary for the winning team to pick the Most Valuable Player for the upcoming awards banquet. Have you given any thought as to who you're gonna give it to?"

Bill chuckled and lied. "I have no idea."

The reporter then put away the note pad, and extended his hand. "Once again, congratulations."

Bill nodded. "Thanks."

The reporter turned and left Bill standing in the middle of the field. The scoreboard still showed the final score; Oilers 18, Knights 14.

Bill looked at it as if he were trying to etch it in his mind. The stands were empty now. Only a few boys remained. They were playing with a miniature football on the other side of the field. The ache in Bill's knee was gone. He twisted it a little. *Hmmm,* he thought, *that's kinda strange.*

Across the field, Mary and Kevin, with little Rebecca in tow, came to him. Kevin was holding the championship trophy, beaming from ear to ear.

Bill turned, put his arm around Mary, and began to walk off the field.

At a distance, Dale was still talking to the two PAL officials. Darrell was nowhere to be seen. Finally, the three men broke off their conversation, and the two officials left.

Dale walked over to Bill. "Bill, can I talk to you for a second?" Dale asked.

Bill replied, "Sure."

He then planted a kiss on his wife's cheek. "I'll be right there," he told her.

Mary, Kevin and Rebecca began walking for the parking lot. Bill stepped aside to talk with Dale.

Bill looked curious. "What's up?"

Dale looked concerned. "We gotta problem."

Now Bill was concerned. "What is it?" he asked.

Dale looked back at him, "You remember those releases?"

Bill nodded, "Yeah, what about 'em?"

Dale continued, "We didn't get 'em for the colored boys."

Bill was sure he was wrong. "Yeah we did."

Dale shook his head. "No, we didn't."

Bill suddenly remembered. The gravity of the situation hit him. "Who knows?"

Dale exhaled. "The PAL rep. He just asked me about 'em. He said someone told him there were no releases on file. He said he's gonna check on it in the mornin'."

Bill rolled his head in agony and buried his face in his hands.

All night long, Bill tossed and turned in bed. It drove Mary crazy. Finally, at the first sight of the morning light, Bill got up. He hadn't been able to sleep all night.

The thought of not turning in the releases had tormented him. As Bill sat at the kitchen table, and attempted to eat his breakfast that morning, his mind raced.

How could they have been so stupid, he thought. In the rush to get the new boys suited up, they forgot about the most important thing—the releases. They had turned in the roster on time, but had totally forgotten about the other league requirement.

The lack of physicals would be forgiven, the lack of releases would not. The physicals, whether or not a child got one or not, was a matter for the parents to decide—but not turning in the releases, that was a matter of league policy.

And as Bill stared at his breakfast, he knew who had turned him in—Darrell. Once again he had been out done by his archrival, and he knew it.

Sitting across from Bill that morning, Kevin was eating a bowl of Wheaties: "The Breakfast of Champions." Mary was sitting at the head of the table, drinking a cup of coffee, and reading the morning newspaper.

She shook the paper, folded it over, and broke the silence. "When asked what he attributed their successful season to, Coach Campbell said, quote 'a low turnout.'"

She lowered the paper. "What'd ya mean by that?"

Bill shook his head. Mary continued to read, "and added he had not yet made up his mind as to who would get the MVP honor to be awarded next Friday night. The Oilers overcame a 14 to nothing half time deficit to beat the previously- undefeated and four- time city champion, McKinley Knights."

She bent the paper back, and showed it to Bill. "Look, it's even got pictures and everything—and look at the title." The headline over the article was "Sleeper wins championship."

Bill looked, but remained unenthusiastic. Mary tried to console him.

She reached out and touched his hand. "Com'on honey, they might take away the title, but they can't take away your victory."

Bill looked at his plate and shook his head. "It just won't be the same," he said.

Mary looked at Kevin. He seemed to agree with Bill.

Bill added, "It just ruins everything. The kids deserve their trophies, patches, and awards. If they take the title away, they won't get any of that."

Finally, Bill got up from the table, and put his half-empty plate into the kitchen sink. He grabbed his jacket off the back of his chair and began to put it on. "I'm meetin' Dale at 8:30. We're gonna see if we can work something out."

As Bill got in his truck that morning, and drove to the police station where the PAL office was, he thought about the last 10 weeks.

From the very start they had faced many obstacles, and now it had come down to this. He couldn't help but feel all their effort had been in vain.

Arriving at the station, Bill got out of his truck and walked inside. Dale was waiting for him. And by the look on his face, he hadn't slept much either. As they entered the league office, a secretary showed them into a nearby room, and closed the door.

The PAL rep had not yet arrived.

On the wall in a large office were two bulletin boards keeping track of the football season, both third- and fourth-grade, and fifth- and sixth-grade leagues. Conspicuously missing on the fifth and sixth grade board was a score under Week Seven, Adams vs. McKinley.

Bill and Dale looked at it, and shook their heads.

After a few minutes, a gentleman entered the room. Bill and Dale stood up. The man was well- dressed, about 45 years old with graying hair.

"Please, have a seat," he said. Bill and Dale sat back down.

The man took his seat behind the desk. "I'm afraid I got some bad news. We checked our files, and we found no releases for fifteen members of your team. Under the rules, that's grounds for forfeiture."

Dale shook his head, and responded first. "You can't just take our season away from us."

The PAL official was resolute. "I'm sorry, but that's the rule."

Bill jumped in. "Look, it's not fair to the kids, they didn't know. Besides, it's my fault."

The PAL official looked like he felt bad about it. "I'm really very sorry, nothing would have happened if someone hadn't pointed it out."

The official then stood up. "You do however have one avenue of recourse."

Bill's eyes brightened a little. "Yeah, what's that?" Bill asked.

The official walked out from behind his desk. "You could petition the league to hold a hearing."

He shook his head and added, "But it probably won't do you much good though. They tend to stick to their rules," he said.

Bill looked at Dale, and then back at the official. "How do we do that?" Bill asked.

With the news they might be able to convene a hearing, Bill told Dale to go on to work. He promised to give him a call once he had found out more.

Later that morning, Bill went home and typed a letter of petition, got back in his truck, drove back downtown to the PAL office, and turned it in.

As he drove home down Market Street, Bill Campbell prayed. He prayed like a desperate man. Two hours later, the PAL office called him at home, and told him the hearing had been granted.

Bill immediately called Dale and gave him the good news. "The meeting is set for tomorrow night," he told him.

On the other end of the line, Dale seemed happy to hear it. "Yessss!" he hollered through the receiver of the phone. "Okay, now what?" Dale asked.

Bill leaned against the kitchen wall. "I tell ya what. You got your roster?"

"Yep," was the reply on the other end of the line.

"You call everyone from Cahill to Milligan. I'll call the rest. Let's see if we can get everyone to show up."

"You thinkin' what I'm thinkin'?" Dale asked.

"Yep," Bill replied.

Later that afternoon Bill called Dale back and the two men exchanged lists. They gave each other the names of those they had not been able to reach. So far, they had only been able to reach about half of the parents, and both men agreed to keep trying.

As Bill hung up the phone, Mary entered the room.

"Who was that?" she asked.

Bill looked at her, and exhaled. "Dale. We got our hearing. It's scheduled for tomorrow night."

By Saturday morning, Bill and Dale reached every parent. All they could do now was wait. It seemed to Bill that the day lasted an eternity.

That evening, Bill and Kevin went to the meeting place early and waited. One by one the Oilers parents arrived, and so did a number of the parents of the Knights, including Darrell.

By 7:30 p.m., the scheduled start time, the room was filled to capacity. The audience was divided into two sections with an aisle between them. Bill and Dale were sitting in the front row left. On the opposite side of the room, Darrell leaned against the wall.

In the middle of the room was a small podium. At the front, was a long table with five white males sitting behind it. They were all PAL officials. The man in the middle tapped the microphone and began to speak. "I'm gonna make this just as short as I can. The issue tonight is whether the city championship, and its title, remain with the Adams Elementary Oilers.

"A motion to strip the title from the Oilers has been filed. Apparently, many of the Oilers players played the entire season without parental consent. As you know, in the past, failure to have consent has resulted in the forfeiture of any and all games in which such players participated. The committee will now take up the complaint. Who's speaking for the Oilers?"

Bill stood up. The official looked over at him. "Do you have a statement?"

Bill moved to the podium. He pulled out a piece of paper.

"Yes I do," Bill said.

The man motioned for Bill to go ahead.

Bill cleared his throat, "I want to offer tonight my sincere apologies to both my players, and to the league, as represented by this committee."

The microphone screeched with feedback. Bill tapped at it with his fingers. As the sound subsided, he continued.

"It was my fault that the release forms were not signed."

Bill looked at many of the Oilers parents, and then back at the committee.

"My kids have worked hard all season, and have overcome more adversity than you'll ever know."

Bill looked across the room at Darrell. Darrell's eyes looked cold. His face was callous. Bill looked back at the committee.

"It would be a shame if my kids had to give up their title for my oversight. I respectfully ask the committee to deny the motion. My kids deserve their championship."

Bill folded up his piece of paper and took his seat. The PAL official nodded. "Who's speaking for the complainant?"

Against the wall, Darrell put up his hand, and walked to the podium. Darrell looked calm, cool, and collected.

He cleared his throat. "Committee members, Mr. Chairman. I can certainly feel empathy for each of the Oilers players, I know we all do, but rules are rules. Everyone else in the league had to play by the rules, so should they. It just wouldn't be right if we were to give them special consideration.

"I ask on behalf of the integrity of the league, that you uphold the rules, and give the title to who it belongs." Darrell nodded at the committee and left the podium.

The chairman looked around, "Does anyone else have anything to add?"

Sitting in the back of the room, a black woman got up from her chair. All eyes turned to her. She had a piece of paper in her hand. She walked to the front of the room and affectionately patted Bill on the shoulder, and whispered something in his ear.

She walked to the committee table, and placed the release form in front of the chairman, and then turned and walked back to her seat.

As she was leaving, right behind her, a black man walked up with his son, and sat his form on top of hers. One by one each black parent approached the table, and presented him their release form.

As the last parent moved back to their seat, the committee members looked moved. The chairman cupped the microphone with the palm of his hand, leaned to his left and then to his right.

The members conferred.

The chairman then straightened up, picked up the release forms, and shaped them up on the table.

"The committee has made their decision. Everything seems to be in order. The title will remain with the Oilers."

The room erupted with cheers. Bill was relieved. He closed his eyes. He then opened them, looked up at the ceiling and smiled. All around him there was much hugging and hand shaking.

On the opposite side of the room, Darrell Phipps looked disappointed. He shook his head a little.

Bill and Kevin never saw the red pickup again. And Bill never did find out who was behind the hate mail—although he said he had a pretty good idea who it was.

But, right after that game, the hate mail stopped coming.

In the middle of the audience, there was another familiar face. It was Frank Felcher. He almost looked like he was smiling. Bill looked at him.

Maybe whoever it was—hated Darrell Phipps more than he hated black people.

Bill didn't know, but one thing was for sure, the city league would never be the same again.

Now it seemed *everyone* wanted a piece of the Carver school district. And as far as Kevin was concerned, that was fine by him.

One week later, the city league held its annual awards banquet. Bill had never been more proud. Each of the boys received his own individual trophy and championship patch.

And the MVP—well it really wasn't a surprise—except to Kevin, a fact that he continued to discuss the following Monday after school.

As he, Randy, and Paul headed home that afternoon, they walked and talked, discussing their achievement. They were walking down a sidewalk three abreast. All three boys were wearing their red-letter jackets.

On each of their left arms was their newest edition. A patch in the shape of a football. The words were clear, "1964 City Champs," Adams Elementary, Fifth & Sixth Grade.

"No. No. No. I should've got the MVP. If it weren't for me, we wouldn't have won." Kevin said.

Randy just shook his head. "Give it up, Campbell."

But Kevin was insistent, "It was my pass that won the game. Really, think about it!"

Randy had heard enough, "Ahhh, shut up Campbell."

Not far away from where the boys were walking, at City Hall, there was a trophy case. In it sat a championship trophy with the inscription, "1964 Adams Oilers."

To the right of it was an MVP plaque, which said, "1964 Charles Taylor Carver Elementary."

The 1965 space was still blank.

About the Author

Scott Staerkel is a 1994 graduate of Regent University, Virginia Beach, Virginia with a M.A. in communication, television programming and production and film emphasis. He has a B.A. in Biblical studies with a minor in military science from Evangel University, Springfield, Missouri where he was also a scholarship athlete. In 1984, he received an early commission as an officer in the U.S. Army, Field Artillery. In the fall of the same year, he was named best defensive back while garnering 1st Team NAIA All District 16 honors. He currently resides in Oklahoma with his five children. He has written several screenplays, and has been optioned twice. This is his first novel.

Printed in the United States
760500005B